Fiction from Modern Chi

This series is intended to showcase new and exciting works by China's finest contemporary novelists in fresh, authoritative translations. It will represent innovative recent fiction by some of the boldest new voices in China today as well as classic works of this century by internationally acclaimed novelists. Bringing together writers from several geographical areas and from a range of cultural and political milieus, the series opens new doors to twentieth-century China.

HOWARD GOLDBLATT

General Editor

Liu Sola

Translated from the Chinese

by Richard King

General Editor, Howard Goldblatt

University of Hawaii Press   *Honolulu*

Chaos

and

All

That

Originally published in Chinese in 1991
by Breakthrough Publications, Hong Kong.

Printed in the United States of America
99 98 97 96 95 94   5 4 3 2 1

Library of Congress Cataloging-in-Publication Data
Liu, Sola, 1955–
　　　[Hun tun chia li ko leng. English]
　　　Chaos and all that / Liu Sola ; translated from Chinese by
　　Richard King.
　　　　　p.　cm. — (Fiction from modern China)
　　　ISBN 0–8248–1617–X (alk. paper). —
　　ISBN 0–8248–1651–X (pbk. : alk. paper)
　　　I. King, Richard. II. Title. III. Series.
　　PL2879.S6H8613 1994
　　895.1'352—dc20　　　　　　　　　　　　　94-9228
　　　　　　　　　　　　　　　　　　　　　　　CIP

Two excerpts from the English translation
appeared in volume 15 (1993) of the journal
Comparative Criticism. Reprinted with the permission of
Cambridge University Press.

University of Hawaii Press books are printed on acid-free
paper and meet the guidelines for permanence and durability
of the Council on Library Resources

Designed by Richard Hendel

Chaos

---

and

All

That

1

Why wasn't I just born an ant?

"Oh my God. Will you look at the little mite – her head's only the size of my fist." Auntie's great-great grandfather was the great-great grandson of an umpteenth-generation descendant of the Great Sage Confucius, so she was surnamed Kong, like him. She put my very first bonnet on her knuckle, and it fit just fine.

The doctors weren't impressed with me either, so they put me in an incubator, like bread going into the oven, to bake for a few days.

When I was ready to go home, the doctor handed Auntie a recipe, and from that point on she was forever fussing about the kitchen, chopping and pulverizing everything she could lay her hands on, concocting soups and purees to pour down my throat. After a month of this she looked me over and pronounced, "This baby is disgustingly fat! Her calves are so chubby you can't even see where her feet begin!" She tweaked my toes through the blubber, chortled "kootchie-koo" and made funny faces, all with no response from me.

"Oh God, it's hopeless. She's gorged herself stupid!" So I was rushed back to hospital for a regimen of physical therapy.

After a month of that I had slimmed down enough that my feet poked out.

After another month I started to grow.

After a year I could cry could laugh could sit could stand could walk could talk could play with my ants.

And after a few more years, when the ants decided to move out, I doused them all with boiling water.

And then there was my family:

Eggs and rice, eggs and rice,
Eat them once and eat them twice;
Open wide, here they come,
Right into your tum-tum-tum.
Poo your pants, poo your pants;
Wash 'em in the river when you get the chance.
Up your pants froggies come,
Bite you on your bum-bum-bum.

Auntie would chant as she walked around the courtyard rocking me in her arms; Mommy and Daddy's snoring wafted out from the North Wing, and the sun lit the swarms of bugs on the crab apple tree.

"What's for dinner, Auntie?"

"Wisteria blossoms."

Wisteria grew in such abundance on the pergola that it blocked out the sun; only the scent of its blossoms was gone. Auntie would knock the furry purple blossoms down with a long pole and scoop them into a wicker basket. Then she would steam them in a pot with salt and garlic. The fragrance was enticing, although I couldn't tell whether it was the garlic or the blossoms that smelled so good. There was a hairy caterpillar on the peach tree; the branches of the date palm that bore the most fruit seemed to grow over the neighbors' fence; and the alley cat with one eye blue and one eye yellow slept under the grape arbor, too lazy to catch mice.

Hey diddle diddle, my pride and joy,
Kong Rong was a good little boy;
Took the littlest pears and plums
And left the big ones for his chums.
Hey diddle diddle, my pride and joy,
Now wasn't he a good little boy?

Auntie made all the stories in our nursery books into rhymes like this. It goes without saying that when we had pears, none of us wanted to take first pick for fear of having to do a Kong Rong.

By now I was growing every time I slept, and as I grew, I dreamed I fell from a steep cliff – down, down – until I woke in terror. Auntie was there. "You've grown some more," she observed.

The turtle clambered out of the fish tank and disappeared into the mud; hairy caterpillars climbed out of the peach blossoms and peered down my neck; the goat stood under the date palm and stared at the cat; the hedgehog stared at the grapes and drooled; the rabbit nibbled the peonies. Auntie had turned the courtyard into a menagerie, and now my brother insisted that he was going to grow wheat in the garden. At Spring Festival Auntie emerged from the cellar bearing a huge melon that had been down there for six months. It was all mushy inside, but Auntie still said, "Eat it while it's fresh." In the main room of the North Wing they put a figurine of the Great Leader that glowed in the dark, and it looked just like my mommy!

"How dare you say such terrible things, little girl!" Auntie glowered at me and just managed not to laugh.

"Little pals, you are the flowers of the nation, the hope of world revolution. You have to learn good manners and proper deportment and when the foreign guests come here tomorrow you go straight over and give them a hug and kiss without being told to – who just farted?" demanded the kindergarten teacher.

The little pals looked at each other.

"Very well then, you must all sniff each others' bottoms. The one with the smelly bottom is the one who farted, and that way the offender will be exposed!"

So we all began to sniff each others' bottoms. Every day the teacher would devise some new version of the exposing-offenders game, and whoever was brave enough to denounce a classmate was a good little child. After one sniff at Song Li's bottom, I knew he was the culprit, but he hissed, "If you tell on me, I'll beat your head in after class!"

So I didn't tell, and when the teacher called on us to expose the offender, Song Li pushed me forward.

"Right then!" the teacher ordered. "Off to the playground and get rid of the smell!" She commended Song Li for daring to wage war on wicked people and evil deeds and instructed all the other little pals that they too must learn to denounce evildoers properly while they were still young.

I didn't have the nerve to tell on Song Li, so I went out into the playground instead of him to air out.

Why do people have to have noses? Nasty ugly bulges sticking out of our faces, always sniffing out revolting smells. The buses were full of grown-ups doing sneaky farts for all they were worth, but no one denounced them. The ones who should have been performing this heroic deed were us little pals, because we were shorter and right up against their bottoms, and we did special sniffing classes in kindergarten. Really good-looking people shouldn't have noses at all.

Mommy took me in for the entrance exam at a posh primary school that had been turning out big shots for hundreds of years, and the first question on the exam was, What do you keep in cages, birds or people?

I received a letter of admission and thereby became the beneficiary of the concern of the state leadership. The leaders even invited our teacher to eat pork hocks with them and sent us cute foreign dolls, which were locked up in display cases in a special exhibition room. The teacher said that the pork hocks served in the leaders' residence at Zhongnanhai were far whiter than the ones you could get in ordinary Peking markets.

When the leaders had their pictures taken, they always made a point of putting on old clothes with big patches and carrying shovels so that everyone would see how hard they worked. But Auntie had herself photographed in a cheong-sam and high heels, which she kept stored in her cut-price treasure chest and which she wouldn't have dreamed of bringing out for everyday.

"I want to be a bluebottle," I wrote in my composition for school. Other essays that got the same grade were pinned up on the board as models; mine and Wazi's were the only exceptions. Her ambition was to be an ambassador's wife. When the teacher read this out in class, everyone laughed at her and she burst into tears. So she gave up on the ambassador's wife idea and wrote in all her essays that she wanted to be a ragpicker instead.

The composition teacher said that my style was elegant enough, but the essay couldn't go up on the wall unless I portrayed the bluebottle as a class enemy. She made me add, "O, that the winter would freeze me! O, that fires would consume me! That the sewer would bear me away! That a flyswatter would slap me! That insecticide would . . ." So it goes.

". . . studied so hard that he stabbed his leg with an awl to stay awake and kept his head up with a rope hung from the rafters . . . ," intoned the form mistress.

". . . the horrors of the old society . . . the theme of this paragraph of our text is . . . ," explained the composition teacher.

"Liu Wenxue sacrificed his precious life to save the commune's — er, yams, wasn't it? Now pay attention when you're writing *yam*. Don't write *yarn* as in *rattling good yarn*," admonished the calligraphy teacher.

"Uncle Lei Feng wrote in his revolutionary diary every day. Could your diaries be published the way his was? If not, then there may be something wrong with your political consciousness," warned the tutor from the Young Pioneers.

Elder brother Russia's finer
Than his little brother China;

Junior bows each time they meet
Can I have something nice to eat?

sang the little girl as she skipped rope.

"Mind what you say. Are you tired of living? Hasn't anyone told you that the Russians are revisionists now?" An old woman rushed over, clouted the child around the head and dragged her home by the ear.

"If the truth be told, every day takes us closer to the grave." In his final class before he retired, the history teacher drew a picture of two people on the blackboard, one farther from the grave – that was us – and one nearer – that was him. The last thing he said to us was, "If you don't believe me, just think about it when you get up in the morning."

I was so scared I couldn't sleep. I boxed my quilt around me like a coffin and imagined going out into the street to beg for food. The people at the end of the alley would sit in their doorway at lunchtime, and their food always smelled more enticing than mine.

"What a little sweetie pie," gushed the woman with the bloodred lipstick on her mouth. She was trying to suck up to my father so that she could ride in his limo and dance with him.

"Put on your school badge!" snapped the duty monitor.

"Eat up all your gristle!" ordered the form mistress.

"Washyourhands washyourhands washyourhands!" yelled Mommy the moment she set foot in the house.

"Children shouldn't listen when grown-ups are talking." Auntie always dragged me away from adult conversations.

"Going to be a change in the weather," said the old pedicab driver at the end of the alley, looking up at the sun and pummeling his legs. Every morning he would sit by the standpipe and scrape the scum off his tongue.

"There's sanitary pads at the store today!" Grown-ups and children rushed off to join the queue.

Then, just as everyone was settling in for their after-lunch nap, there came a voice loud enough to scale the highest walls and be heard in the North Wing: "Grind your knives; sharpen your scissors!"

I couldn't be an ant; I had this great nose that sniffed out nasty smells, and I couldn't be a bluebottle and be swept away down the sewer. I had revolutionary aspirations and a sound physique – I was healthy in body, mind, and spirit. All I needed was a red kerchief, and I was practically ready to shake hands with the leaders. "Two-thirds of the world's foreigners are languishing in despair and need us to go and save them. . . . American imperialism manufactures stiletto heels and the twist to poison the people's souls." The Great Leader and Poet wrote,

> On this tiny globe
> A few flies dash themselves against the wall
> The sound is sometimes chilling
> And sometimes like sobbing.

We lived bang in the center of the world, the place where all people longed to be.

Mommy told Granny, "If you go to the netherworld in an old-style longevity suit and there's a revolution going on down there, then they'll call you a landlord's wife and beat you up."

"Well then, I'll have to be burned." Granny had always been dead set against cremation, but now she went off the idea of burial in a longevity suit with equal determination. She ate a hearty breakfast of oil fritters and bean milk and died at noon with a smile on her face.

* * *

Was this writing a novel? Huang Haha stared blankly at what she had written. She hadn't thought that she had lived long enough to be doing any such thing. But she'd had this sudden urge to write one anyway, and a mass of material had come gushing out of her mind, a ragbag of half-told stories, half-formed ideas and half-remembered incidents. She forgot them when she was trying to write, and then they leaped out at her when she was distracted, as if determined to drag her away from her daily life in London.

"If you keep on wearing that sweater with pictures of goats on it, you might end up turning into a goat yourself," she imagined herself saying to the young man nodding off opposite her in the stuffy warmth of the Tube. For some reason the sight of his little goats made her feel sick, and she thought up a string of insults to hurl at him. She knew that they weren't really aimed at him – so who were they for? Anyway, Haha had it in for everyone right now.

Maybe it was because of the weather.

Haha was used to the way things were in Peking. Here in London there was no difference between the seasons, no variety or distinction, no yin and yang, and the people, like their weather, were bland and colorless. She'd arrived just in time for another downpour, and – what with the rain and the people on the street – it was like walking into a B movie. No sooner had the women decided it was all right to put on skirts over bare legs than there was a cold snap that was enough to give you arthritis.

Still, London was a nice enough place. People were flocking to it from all parts of the world, searching for freedom. More and more of them all the time, so that this freedom was going up in price and became more elusive the later you arrived. At least that was what Old Gu was always telling Haha.

Haha had come here to go to college. Someone had helped her find a cheap place to rent, and there she stayed apart from her time in class at college. She had no real friends in London. The other Chinese students were all rushed off their feet, and the natives weren't in the habit of standing around and passing the time of day. Because Haha had a scholarship, money wasn't a problem, but she was so bothered by all those things gushing out of her mind that she was practically oblivious to the delights that London offered. She even lost track of why it was she had come here in the first place. She rattled around her flat for hours on end babbling to herself, her moods swinging from one extreme to the other. Things she barely understood wove themselves into a net that entangled her as she went to class and wrapped itself round her on dates with her boyfriend. Everything but Haha herself was outside the net – the things she was supposed to learn in class, Michael, people who wanted to get to know her.

She was trapped in the net and enchanted by it. The French window that faced her desk had louver doors instead of curtains, and every night as she pulled them shut she would repeat the street cry she had heard in Peking as a child when the old stores were boarded up for the night: "Shutters away, hey!" They'd been everywhere, those old-fashioned stores, but then suddenly they were gone, replaced by glass-fronted boutiques with mannequins in the windows. What a thrill it had been to stand out in the street after the change first took place and gawk at the bright-colored tiles and neon signs! Back then, the residents of the old courtyards had wanted nothing so much as the chance to move into an apartment building. It wasn't until they moved into their new flats and found they had nothing to do all day that they realized what it was like without that down-to-earth feeling. The sights and sounds of Peking were all the more evocative for Huang Haha here at the other end of the earth, and she felt nostalgic for the 1960s, when two cents would buy a candyman, and fifty would buy a big package of fried biscuits or almond shortcakes frosted with red sugar. She longed for the coarse yellow toilet paper – you had to try and rub it smooth before you used it, and when you'd finished, you had to rub your bottom to stop the itching – for the queues to buy sanitary pads, for tiny goldfish, for crickets, for the slab cake that old men would cut and sell by the piece. She even remembered with affection the way the vendors would hawk and spit. When they blew their noses, they would pinch off the snot and wipe their fingers on their trousers before picking up another piece of the cake.

Haha sat by the window looking out at the street. The leisured ladies of London were taking the air, their complacent faces redolent with the pomp and grandeur of British culture. This took her back to the streets of her childhood, to the revolutionary grannies of Peking who seemed to find themselves and their society more radiant than the sun. They would strut up and down the street, chests out, beady eyes vigilant, and woe betide you if you got in their way or if they didn't like the look of you. The final line of the tirade would always be, "Just don't forget this is the great capital city, all right?" The ladies of London only had to say "Don't forget . . ." for their children to denounce them as racists, imperialists, or conservatives. Better for them just to smile benignly at the world, shake their heads, exchange knowing looks, and then return to their refined appreciation of the pleasant weather. Londoners restored antiquities, displayed them prominently, and left them alone; the people of Peking picked up the shards of their past and either sold them off or smashed them for the hell of it. It was enough to set Haha wondering about the meaning of life.

London. Peking. Classical sculpture. Opera. Nationality. Peking Man. *Anna Karenina.* Wang Baochuan. The criteria for making judgments that had been drummed into her from infancy were no use at all when she actually had to make up her mind about anything. Those criteria were all about victory and defeat, right and wrong. Everything she did was in competition with the people of London. It was like being in a great wrestling ring, where it was either win or die. If the Asian sages were not king, it was because the Western aggressors had usurped their crown. But in practice the images of the combatants were so blurred that she couldn't tell them apart anymore: Does *The Story of the Stone* really have to be greater than the works of Shakespeare? Must the Chinese poet Li Po be greater than Goethe? Do all my essays have to be stupendously brilliant? If I make a mistake, does that make me a failure? How do I get to be what I'm supposed to be?

Haha would fill whole pages writing out the two words *right* and *wrong.* These two words had been with her all her life; everything she had done was stamped with one or the other of them. No matter how much needless conflict and anguish it caused her, she still used *right* and *wrong* to punish herself and others.

Not that she was a pessimistic person. It was Daddy who had come up with the name Haha, hoping that with such a name she would rise joyfully above the ordinary. As for him, in spite of a lifetime spent parading the virtues of transcendence, he still ended up taking his life during the Cultural Revolution. Mommy had always said that "a resolute Communist Party member would never contemplate suicide." Daddy's actions had done away with any claim he might have had to such noble status and had landed Haha and her mother in the soup at the same time. Still, Haha was determined to remain optimistic at all costs, or at least to put on a good show of optimism, and so prove herself as cheerful as her name and worthy of the auspicious future the fortune-teller had predicted for her as a child: "Her face is full; her achievements will be abundant."

"It's no big deal. I'm fine." At least, that was what she told everyone else. However many rights and wrongs she wrote at her desk, she still had a name to live up to.

*　*　*

"Oh my God. It's going to pot. The kids are all turning into little rebels!" wailed Auntie, waving the frying pan.

Nineteen hundred and sixty-six wasn't just some random number picked out of thin air, nor were the extraordinary events of the year bearing that number taking place on some idle whim. If the earth was really the revolving sphere that the Teacher said it was, then it was only to be expected that the things that took place where we were in the morning could happen in America the same evening. Just look at the papers! They were full of reports that a great and unprecedented Cultural Revolution was about to break out, and then what do you see when you turn on the TV in the evening but Americans marching in the streets in a Cultural Revolution of their own! We were taught that "every word of the Great Leader is a roll of the war drum," and sure enough, there on the TV were Africans shouting, "Long live Chairman Mao!" and beating time on tom-toms. Of course, they just might have been actors dressed up and putting on a show for our benefit, but surely the foreigners we saw on the news queuing for copies of the *Selected Works* couldn't *all* be acting, could they? It was said that everyone in the world had a copy of the Little Red Book, the only exception being the old man who sat by the standpipe scraping the scum off his tongue. He said it cost too much, but then he turned out to be a member of the landlord classes, so what could you expect? In the morning the sun rose on our side of the earth, and in the evening it shone on the other half; any place it wanted to make red became red, and who was there that could resist its glow? When the Great Leader reviewed the Red Guards – my brother among them – resplendent in their military fatigues, army belts, and red armbands, it seemed that our euphoria had spread right through the world. Apparently British students were growing their hair long and shouting slogans in the streets. Only they should have got their facts straight before they started to make revolution – as far as we were concerned, long hair and high heels, like cats, dogs, and rabbits, were all class-enemy stuff, and growing your hair long was like asking to have your throat slit. Foreigners didn't seem quite able to comprehend the "overall direction"; maybe it was something to do with the way the sun shone on them. The world was not quite as easily manipulated as was our globe at home.

"I want to be a Red Guard too." I longed for the prestige of wearing fatigues, belt, and armband.

"Piss off," said my brother.

"What's a little kid like you doing swearing?" Auntie scowled at him.

"Do you read Lu Xun?" Brother countered.

"Oh my God. I just happen to have read everything except Lu Xun!" Auntie stuck out her tongue at him.

"Didn't you read Lu Xun's essay on the swearword *His mother's* ———— ?" Brother was getting quite worked up. Auntie and I glanced at each other, both at a loss. They hadn't told us about this one in elementary school.

"If a real authority like Lu Xun says that *His mother's* ———— is part of the national heritage, how can you make revolution without it?" Brother's neck bulged defiantly.

Auntie didn't back down. She made a little officer suit in a delicate shade of dogshit brown for me to wear instead of fatigues with epaulets like my brother and his crowd. I wasn't sure if it looked more like a nationalist uniform or a communist one, but when my brother saw it he was meaner to me than ever. Well fuck you anyway, Big Brother. I tried it on, struck some revolutionary poses in front of a mirror, and decided I was a natural to be a dancer.

I danced my way to the front door. Auntie called after me, "Don't be late coming home."

"Don't you fucking boss me around!" There! I'd finally managed to say it, although I didn't think I'd used the word to very good effect.

"Little brat! I should take a strap to you!" My mother appeared in the courtyard. She was wearing a mannish Mao suit that made her waist look slimmer and showed off her breasts and hips. I fled.

The street was packed with Red Guards. As I stepped

over the threshold of the big red gate and out into the alley, the first thing I saw was the old tongue-scraping pedicab driver. Now he was an old landlord being beaten up by Red Guards, his nose bloody and his face bruised. The simple working man of a few days ago had suddenly been transformed into a member of the exploiting classes, in just the same way that he must have changed from landlord to pedicab driver at some time in the past. Apparently the Red Guards had searched his house and discovered a strange chart on which was written the names of hexagrams used for divination. Some people said it was superstition; others that it was a counterrevolutionary slogan; still others that it was an old land deed. Finally it was decided that his most heinous offense was scraping off all that yucky stuff in a deliberate attempt to turn the stomachs of the revolutionary masses, so that the revolutionary masses would be so grossed out by the sight of him at work on his tongue that they wouldn't be able to practice correct oral hygiene themselves. He was "unrepentant despite his great crimes," and the Red Guards made him eat dirt, so that his landlord-class tongue would become physically the piece of stinking dog shit it was politically. They also gave his wife a yin-yang haircut, one side left long and the other side shaved bald and shiny. When I saw him crawling along the ground licking up the dirt, his head smeared with blood and muck, his face so beaten up that he looked like a ghoul, my knees started knocking and I felt like throwing up. I'd rather have watched him scraping a pound of scum off his tongue.

I skirted unsteadily around a crowd of Red Guards about my brother's age – junior high school students – and pretty tough looking. But I still wanted to go along to school with them, to see if I could join the Red Guards too. What made a Red Guard? An old-style army uniform bleached by many washings, a webbing belt, a red armband bearing the words *Red Guard* in the scrawly writing of the Supreme Commander, basketball shoes, and a military backpack. Even the

Great Leader himself wore a red armband, and when he waved his hand at Tiananmen a million Red Guards wept their hearts out as if by some hormonal reaction. Later on we were all conditioned to burst into tears the moment He appeared on the screen. He was divine, and the revolutionary tides of the world rose and fell at His command. If even *He* wanted to be a Red Guard – their leader, that is – how could anyone, even a newborn, resist the urge to wear the red armband? Besides, I was all of eleven years old. I wasn't always going to be trailing along behind my brother and his friends, selling their pamphlets or "maintaining revolutionary traffic discipline" by declaiming slogans on buses: things like "Make a resolution to fear no hardships, overcome ten thousand difficulties and win final victory." I'm not sure which genius came up with the idea of having elementary schoolkids bawling revolutionary songs and declaiming Directives from On High to complete strangers on the street and in the buses. We sang and shouted ourselves hoarse, but no one ever applauded. Whoever's lousy idea it was, they made us look like a bunch of idiots.

"Hey, what are you doing here?" Little Ding asked me in the school yard.

"I've come to join the Red Guards." I looked over to the classroom building. Classes had been suspended long ago, and the only person still around was the old commissionaire who watered the flowers.

"Me too." She was chewing a toffee again, and her front teeth were black with decay. Back when we were in school, she used to show off by sticking a piece of wire right through her teeth to prove how rotten they were.

"Do you know what you have to do to join?"

"People like us with good families just fill out a form – " She caught herself. "Your family's got no problems, eh?"

"Course not."

"Then you're fine." When she grinned, I could see the bits of toffee sticking to her black teeth.

I knew she'd be fine – her father was a general and her mother a doctor assigned to care for the state leaders in Zhongnanhai. Her teeth were living proof of her mother's fine quality of neglecting personal matters for the common good, just as my mother had got my own birth out of the way prematurely so she could get back to serving the revolution sooner.

Our school's only Red Guard organization was named 8–18 to commemorate August 18, the day that the Great Leader had reviewed a Red Guard parade. The 8–18 group was headquartered in the classroom building in what had been the fifth-grade classroom. As we peered around the door of the classroom, there was a crack like a whiplash. A boy with big round eyes was standing in wait for us, flicking a leather belt.

"What're you doing here?" He had one foot on the chair.

"We've come to sign up for the Red Guards," I said. Little Ding hadn't finished her toffee.

"You expect to be a Red Guard looking like that?" He glared at Little Ding's mouth. Suddenly I noticed that we were surrounded by Red Guards, boys and girls in faded military fatigues, all students from grades higher than ours.

I tried to draw myself up to my full height. The problem was that I couldn't stand up too straight because I thought that this might make me look too much like a kid in primary school. To look like a grown-up you have to slouch a bit, but then to look like a revolutionary you have to thrust your chest forward and buttocks back. I sat down.

"Who told you you could sit down?" His eyes popped out even farther. "Stand up!"

I stood up. Nothing for it, I'd just have to be a primary schoolkid. There I was, hands behind my back, chest out, buttocks back.

He eyed me up and down. "How old are you?"

"Eleven."

"Eleven! A fucking eleven-year-old and she wants to be a

Red Guard." His neck bulged. He couldn't have been more than twelve himself.

I just stood there, chest out, tummy in, buttocks back, pigeon-toed, submissive and attentive.

"Class origin?" he snapped.

"Revolutionary cadre!" I held my head high.

"Revolutionary military!" Little Ding's voice was louder still.

"Hmm." The boy took his foot off the chair and went over to the desk to pick up some forms. "Can you say fuck?"

Neither of us said a word. All that practice at home for nothing.

He cracked his belt on the chair again. "Got enough guts to beat the shit out of people?"

Silence again. He had us cowed.

"Dare you protect the revolutionary red regime with your life blood?" His eyes opened wider than ever.

Not a word. I was thinking of the old tongue scraper.

"What's got into you? Lost your tongues?" He started to thrash the table with his belt.

"Just go home, okay? You're too young, you're no use for anything, having you tagging along would be a pain in the neck," said a girl from the fifth grade.

Piss off, I thought. That was what my brother had said to me.

Little Ding and I fled from the classroom. As we left, we heard them yelling and arguing inside.

"Where did we go wrong?" I asked her.

"Can't you see? It's 'cause we can't swear properly."

"So what do we do?"

"What's stopping us? Let's practice."

"How do we do that?"

"Come on." She pulled me over to the corner. "I'll say it first; then you go after me, and we'll see who does best."

"Okay."

"Fuck," she said.

"Fuck," I responded. So far so good.

"Fuck you."

"Fuck you."

"Fuck your mother."

"Fuck your mother."

"Fuck your mother's eggs!"

"Fuck your mother's eggs!" Still no problem.

"Fuck your mother's bloody eggs!"

"Fuck your mother's bloody eggs!"

"Roll your mother's fucking eggs!"

"Roll your mother's fucking eggs!"

"You fucking bastard!"

"You fucking bastard!"

"Your mother's – " She checked herself in midflow.

"Your mother's WHAT?" I was waiting.

She tried again. "Your mother's – " She started to giggle.

"Go on, say it!"

"Your mother's – " She whispered the last word: "Cunt."

"Your mother's – " It was no good. I couldn't do it.

"Watch me, I can yell it to the whole school yard." Giggling uncontrollably, she put her legs slightly apart and braced herself like someone about to dive into a swimming pool.

I held my breath.

"Your mother – your mother's – mother's – mother's – mother's CUNT-T-T-T!" The final word exploded like a grenade, reverberating around the school yard. All the members of the 8–18 Red Guard brigade stuck their heads out of the window and gaped at us.

2

The most essential qualification for being a Red Guard was that you had to be able to say to people's faces the kinds of thing you usually only find written on toilet walls. Mommy said that it was only people from the worst families with the thickest skins that would come out with things like that.

When Brother heard her mention thick skin, he offered this story: There was once a man who died and went to hell. When he reached the netherworld, he asked King Yama why he hadn't grown a beard. King Yama told him, "You were actually supposed to have an inch of beard, but the skin on your face was two inches thick so the whiskers never managed to stick through." Brother obviously wasn't bothered by the prospect of not growing a beard and didn't mind throwing in some choice vocabulary of his own. What's more important in life anyway, glory or facial hair?

Auntie said, "You kids needn't think you're through the worst of it, there's things ahead of you yet."

That was true enough: everyone seemed to be doing their best to make life difficult for us. After gym class there was walking, running, talking, pole climbing, parallel bars, handstands, swimming, dancing, writing, arithmetic – all so that you could have a report card that said you weren't some kind of bonehead. The reason the doctors had put me through all that physical therapy when I was a baby was simply so that I would be quicker at standing, walking, running, talking, thinking, cursing others, and being cursed.

"Work out till you drop!" hissed the boy as he pumped weights.

"Work out!" shouted the captain of the Young Pioneers.

"Let's go outside and work out!" yelled the two boys as they squared off against each other.

All human life was reduced to one thing – working out.

"Fuck!" Behind a locked door I worked out in front of the mirror, practicing facial expressions. As my mouth slowly opened, the eyes in the mirror grew rounder.

"*Fuck!*" Now the eyes in the mirror narrowed to slits.

"Fuck *you!*" I really worked at it this time, teeth clenched, lips thin, eyes staring more than ever. You had to practice to the point where everybody would be afraid of you as soon as you said the words. But when I said the *you* bit, I noticed that I still had dimples in my cheeks. Hey! I was getting to look like that actress, you know, what's-her-name! "So what's the big deal about being an actress?" Brother sneered. "They all look the same anyway." Auntie told Brother, "You need to have the right look to act. Haha's got it, and you haven't. Go on, Haha; give us your militant heroine again!" So I did the revolutionary glowering at the class enemy, complete with bulging neck and popping eyes. Auntie clapped her hands and hooted with laughter.

"Cunt!" This was the worst word I knew. The face in the mirror blushed scarlet and looked all around. There was no one there, of course. Even the old ground beetle on the wall didn't come out to listen.

He was a dirty great black beetle, clinging to the white-washed toilet walls with hairy feet. Often he would work his way along the wall to a point above the toilet bowl, so that you might well see him if you looked up while you were sitting there. He never avoided people, but we all avoided him, and I got so I couldn't shit when he was around.

The house was too old and too big. I was the first generation of our family to be born there, but the beetles, rats, lizards, millipedes, and ants could well have been there for hundreds of generations. Auntie told us that the human occupants of the house had changed with every change of dynasty: the previous master of the house had killed someone here and then run off to Taiwan with the nationalists; the one before him had committed treason and got himself executed; the one before *him* had fallen out with President Yuan Shikai; the one before *him* had been an imperial eunuch at the court of the Dowager Empress Cixi; and the one before *that* . . . Daddy said it might just be that there had originally been a slaughterhouse on this site, or maybe a graveyard. Auntie told him he shouldn't say such terrible things. I said that for sure the rats and beetles hadn't moved house. Brother said straight away that he wondered how bad the toilet had smelled back then.

"That's quite enough of that," Auntie ruled. "People haven't always been as picky about that sort of thing. Anyway, the ancients wouldn't wash and poo in the same room. Think about lovely Empress Yang emerging from the bath."

"For God's sake!" Brother complained. "What's Empress Yang in the bath got to do with anything?" Auntie looked hurt.

"That," Mommy interrupted, "was the decadent lifestyle of the oppressor classes."

"But we have worker uncles looking after the boiler for us here, don't we?" I asked.

"That's different," Mommy replied. "Daddy has made great contributions to the revolution."

Actually Daddy wasn't at all fond of washing; he preferred to rub his back on a doorpost if he had an itch. I thought it was much more fun to go to the public baths with the other kids from the street.

Mommy said, "How come every generation of this family acts like a bunch of peasants?"

I didn't like the house. The rooms were big and dingy,

and the green paint had flaked off the walls in patterns that looked like gaping mouths with bared fangs. Size was the only thing it had going for it. Big tiled buildings, big courtyards, big red doorways, big ornamental walls, big red-lacquered pillars, big stairways, big lizards, big beetles, big caterpillars, big rats, big millipedes, big black shadows.

"Auntie, why's our house so uncomfortable? Granny Wang's house next door has the bed in the first room you go into. Her home's cozy and it smells nice."

"You're no good for anything, little girl. We'd better just send you off to the countryside and have done with it."

"Will we eat millet cakes and have wood fires?"

"You're going to have to learn how to take care of yourself. How can you live in a village if you can't even wash a hanky?"

Auntie taught me how to make noodles: first make the dough, then slap it flat and roll it out into slabs with the rolling pin, then roll it flatter and bigger, until your palms are red and itchy. Then pile up the great slabs of dough and cut them into strips, and there's your noodles. Auntie said I'd have to practice making noodles for a week before I'd be of any use, and then we'd make the dough wrappers for *jiaozi*. Then we'd make steamed bread, and *then* I could learn how to catch rats with a broom.

That was cat's work. Rats were a lot quicker than I was. Auntie and I, each of us brandishing a bamboo besom, chased a little rat around and around the courtyard until it got dizzy, and then Auntie pinned it with her broom and ground the broom down until the animal was dead. When she lifted her broom to examine our prey, we saw that the little creature's body was a mass of stab wounds from the bamboo spikes. Auntie still wasn't through with it; she jabbed two more holes through it with a pair of fire tongs.

"Poor little thing," I said.

"Its bones are still soft," she said.

Next Auntie shoved the cat down a hole in the floorboards to catch rats. The cat just wasn't up for it. It stood at the entrance to the hole and wailed all night, warning all the rats that we were after them. Auntie cut the cat off food for three days to punish it and then stuffed it back down the hole. "You can't coddle 'em; ratting is what cats are for." That cat had kittens, and those kittens had kittens of their own, and each generation was even less willing to go ratting than the one before. My schoolmate's cat was fed on fish and milk and ran away and hid whenever a mouse appeared. Auntie disapproved: "Tsk, tsk, it's no wonder the papers say we're going revisionist." She tried harder than ever to get the cat under the floorboards.

When the revolutionary rebellion was getting going, the revolutionary antirevisionist brigades launched a campaign to combat revisionism by killing all the cats they could lay their hands on. Auntie got really upset: "Oh my God. So what are we supposed to do when the place gets overrun with rats?" Then she felt sorry for the cats: "What did they ever do to anyone to get treated like that?" Some of the cats got firecrackers stuffed up their asses, which blew them to smithereens; some of them were sentenced to the "hot pillar" and got burned to a crisp; and some were tossed down from high buildings and splattered to a pulp on the ground below.

Auntie put our cat into her shopping basket, covered it with a cloth, and took it out of the city for safety. When she got to a place where there were no people, she let the cat out. It stretched lazily and yawned, and then started to follow Auntie back home. Auntie moaned, "Bloody cat!" put it back in the basket, and brought it home. Next day she took it farther away. When she let the cat out of the basket, it stared at her reproachfully, and she brought it back home again. The third day Auntie took it still farther, right into the mountains, and she left it under a tree. Auntie didn't even dare to glance at it; she just scuttled home as fast as her legs would carry her. The cat neither cried nor followed her.

A few months later a huge wild cat appeared on the roof. Everyone said it looked just like our cat Blossom, but this one resisted all attempts to get it down. Auntie said it had gone back to nature and toughened up, and certainly it was several times bigger. I said it must be nicer to be a wild cat than a tame one; domestic cats were always having to be obliging, and even then they might get stuffed down a rat hole or have firecrackers stuffed up their bums.

"Fuck!" It took a lot of effort to get the word out, and I still wasn't sure when would be the right time to use it.

Ratatat! Someone was knocking at the bathroom door.

"You shitting gold bricks in there or what? Come and help me take care of your brother. His group made him take the lead in destroying the Four Olds. He's burning his stamp collection."

But those stamps were Brother's pride and joy! Even the rejects from his collection were exciting enough to be displayed in my school's showcases.

I dashed out.

They were already ablaze. All his sets of stamps, those lovely colored triangles, squares, and diamonds – illustrations of children's stories from all around the world, images of great men, pictures of flora and fauna, historic sites and great events of the past that might have been forgotten but for the stamps – all were going up in flames, burned to little ashes that floated up and then came down to rest on Brother's white basketball shoes or on his red armband. Tears were streaming down his face. Auntie began to sob in sympathy, and I could find no words of comfort.

"Fuck it!" I said suddenly. Not loudly, but I said it. Auntie's little eyes widened and she stopped crying. Brother didn't even notice.

* * *

For Huang Haha, recalling days gone by was like taking stimulants. Things that had happened in those days, even the most piddling and insignificant things, were real *events;* as for now, she hardly knew if she was alive or dead. Her problem was that all the time she was living in the present tense she still imposed on it the feelings of the past tense, which made the present tense seem drab and colorless. So while she was having dinner with Michael, the candles on the table would spark memories: "If you'd taken a lamp in, you'd have seen the maggots all over the place. The floor was covered with them; really, you couldn't help standing on them. In the spring the maggots would all turn into chrysalides and crunch under your feet. Sometimes when you were squatting, you'd see the corpses of pigs, dogs, and chickens that had drowned and resurfaced, floating in the shit. If you didn't watch out, you might fall in yourself, like taking a dive into a swimming pool!"

Michael would join in her laughter, digesting the thought of the Chinese village toilets as he ate his curry, rice, and chapatis.

"How come it doesn't affect your appetite?" Haha complained.

"Makes me hungrier than ever." Michael wanted to impress her with his nonchalance. "Looks like shit, doesn't it?" he said, pointing at the dish of curry. That finished any desire Haha might have had for food.

Haha felt misunderstood. "Don't you realize how sensitive I am about shit?"

"Pardon me, I'm sure; I thought you were over that kind of thing by now. Besides, isn't everyone sensitive about shit?" Michael made a joke of his apology.

"It's not the same!" she insisted.

"Pardon me," he apologized again.

Michael was crazy about her in those days. He hung on her every word.

"What if I'd married a peasant?" she asked, tweaking his beard.

He put his mouth on hers to shut her up.

As soon as she had the chance to draw breath she asked, "And what if I'd caught leprosy?"

He undid her buttons.

"Fat was worth money. In our village they measured the value of brides by their weight," she said, looking at her own flesh.

Michael was impatient to offer his heart to this mysterious lover who had endured so much. There were tears in his eyes as he embraced her. From underneath his body, she asked him, "You ever heard of snail fever?"

Michael was Haha's teacher at college in London. It had been love at first sight, or, as the Peking lowlifes would say, it was like the turtle eye to eye with the green bean – the ideal match. Michael found Haha exotic and inscrutable; she liked him for his maturity and worldliness – he could be father and brother to her as well as lover. Michael's love for her gave her a platform from which she could flaunt her eloquence and her charm. She talked and he listened; she performed and he watched. She could use her past to overshadow both their presents. The only thing that made her less happy than about their relationship was Michael's fiancée.

Yes, Michael had a fiancée. Nobody had actually seen her, but everyone knew that there was such a person. In addition to her, Michael also had a constant stream of girlfriends. When he was with Haha, he broke off with the other girlfriends; only his fiancée remained silently but unassailably in place. Young people in London didn't see this kind of thing as being any big deal. When Michael was with Haha he would call his fiancée, and, when he was with his fiancée, he would call Haha. The other woman. She had always been taught that this kind of person was like a thief, but she felt that in their case it wouldn't be fair to herself if she wasn't a thief. After all, Michael had told her that he and she were a match made in heaven, and, if heaven ordains something, it can't be stealing to take it, can it?

"It's no good. Let's just forget the whole thing," she said to Michael.

"That's no good, we can't just forget it," said Michael to her.

"It's getting more complicated all the time."

"It's the most straightforward thing there is."

"How so?"

"I love you."

"This business with you and Michael is a real mess," said Dongxia. Dongxia was from Peking like Haha, and they often took walks together and talked things over. Dongxia was doing an M.A. in engineering, and her husband was still in Peking. She'd struggled through four years in London without him. Now that he'd finally been awarded the scholarship that they had been longing for, she had celebrated by buying new clothes for the first time since her arrival, which meant that she didn't smell bad anymore.

"It's simple enough; I love him, and he loves me." Haha managed to make her voice sound casual and matter-of-fact, even as the words *right-wrong, right-wrong, right-wrong* flashed through her mind.

"He has a fiancée, right? I heard she's ten years younger than him and filthy rich." Dongxia was sucking at a piece of fruit. She swallowed what was in her mouth, and without waiting for Haha to reply she went on: "So either find a way of splitting them up or else break off with him yourself. Don't let things get more confused than they are now, or there's going to be all sorts of talk." She spat seeds decisively onto the ground.

"Everything in life is a mess, and I'm not about to live my life just so that people will say nice things about me." If only I could really believe what I'm saying, she thought.

"Have it out with him. If it's okay, then go ahead. If not then drop it, and don't waste your energy on him." She let another seed go.

What did it mean, wasting your energy?

"Wanna screw?" said a young guy walking past Dongxia. He didn't even look at her.

Haha used to talk to Old Gu, too. They had moved in the same circles when they were in Peking.

"Human beings must exercise restraint." Old Gu looked at her out of the corner of his eye. He claimed that he had vanquished vulgar desires.

"If you've vanquished vulgar desires, what are you doing in London?" Haha felt that she knew Old Gu; sometimes it occurred to her that if she were Old Gu's girlfriend, she would be able to avoid misunderstandings, conflicts, and mysteries, but without mystery there's no spark, and if there's no spark, then there's no passion; without passion there's no trouble; and if there's no trouble, there's nothing at all.

Perhaps the world really did have nothing at all to offer Old Gu. He would hold forth on the subject of sex, his face a study of saintly detachment and invulnerability. Even his mouth scarcely moved as he discussed sex in the most arcane and erudite terms. If there were a group of people there, he would become even more eccentric and austere than usual, so that whoever he was talking to would finish up feeling as impure as a pig or a dog.

Whoever fell for him was right out of luck. He maintained his facade of restraint all the time, but the moment he got the message that someone fancied him he would turn on the self-control more than ever. The thing that terrified him more than anything else was showing his emotions, and it was only with a woman like Haha, who understood him completely and didn't desire him in the slightest, that he could relax. He would take off his shirt, bare his shoulders, pat his lean stomach, and show off his sinewy muscles.

"A foreigner . . . hmm . . . it's natural to want a bit of fun . . ." He had a habit of leaving sentences half-finished.

". . . I suppose it's all right as long as you don't catch AIDS." He plucked a stray hair out of his writing brush with slim fingers and stared dispassionately at the brush tip.

Haha should have known she was asking for trouble talking to Old Gu about love. As far as he was concerned, Westerners were promiscuous AIDS carriers, and Asians were little homebodies. Nothing was worth getting worked up about, and if you said to him, "I love him," or "I love her" and all that stuff, he would smile patronizingly and reply, "Be your age! You're acting like a little kid!"

He would use this humor of his to destroy your self-respect, so that in the end you too would think you were an idiot. He had known passion himself: once he had fought a duel with kitchen cleavers over some girl, but, as he got older and more experienced, *love* and *stupidity* became synonyms in his lexicon.

"Okay, okay. You're a big girl now; you need someone to settle down with."

"I never said a bloody word about settling down. Don't give me that shit! Why does everything have to be for a purpose?" Haha resented the way Old Gu had simplified her problem.

"So how do you want to look at it? Love? Okay, just go ahead; be in love – leave it at that. Or else get married – isn't that the same as settling down?"

"But I'm the other bloody woman!"

"Didn't you say you wanted a bit more excitement in your life?" Old Gu laughed.

Haha was so mad she had to laugh, too.

"Go ahead and do it. Be the other woman, or the third woman, or the fourth or fifth; you'll have more fun that way than doing nothing." He got up to make tea.

"I want to end it with him," Haha said seriously to Old Gu's back.

"Then break it off. Have a good meal; that beats anything." He made the tea and blew at the leaves floating at the top of his mug.

Haha stood up. "Tell me what I ought to do," she said, hoping to talk more seriously with him.

"You want me to do it *all* for you?" He stared at her with mock earnestness.

Haha went over and kicked him. Then she walked out.

She heard his parting shot as she left: "Women!"

3

Women! What about men?

"With a mighty rumble like a peal of thunder, Meng Jiangnü's tears washed away the Great Wall."

> . . . My father bade me take another man,
> But Ping returned in honor to our home;
> Baochuan his wife is pure and undefiled. . . .

This was how it was supposed to be; if the husband was to return in honor, then the wife must be pure and undefiled. The upright magistrate Judge Bao condemned the disloyal husband Chen Shimei; the bandit hero Wu Song killed the adulteress Pan Jinlian. When Chinese people want to say that what's done can't be undone, they use the popular saying, "The raw rice has been made into porridge." But what's the raw rice here, and what's the porridge? Do you *have* to eat the porridge? What if you don't feel hungry? Aren't we supposed to make revolution economically?

What's right? What's wrong?

Haha got out of her chair and sat up on the table, feeling that the extra altitude might clear her mind. Finally she found herself fascinated by the dustbins on the street and still as confused as ever.

Of course, as far as Old Gu was concerned, women had minimal IQs. And the little intelligence they had went into shopping. In high antiquity, when there weren't so many stores, women had put their intelligence to work managing the family budget, and their remaining energies were for the kitchen and the bedroom. And then? "I tell you, as time has gone by they've gotten to be more and more trouble." This was Old Gu's bottom line on women. Haha knew that Old Gu was just needling her; she also realized that her life would be a lot easier if she played dumb a bit more. What men most like to hear women say is "I don't know."

She sat cross-legged on the table and looked down at the dustbins. Michael really had split up with her this time; the passion that made him say, "That's no good, we can't just forget it," had cooled. Haha had nothing to feel guilty about anymore, since the burden of being a thief had now been shifted to some *other* other woman. And his fiancée was still sitting securely at home, waiting for him to call her from the other woman's house. Even though she was no longer the other woman, Haha still wanted to understand what it was that there had been between them. She had been serious about the affair at first, almost thinking that she had found the man she could settle down with. Then, all of a sudden – bang – here she was sitting alone in a sinking ship, trying to understand what the hell relationships were: Dustbins? Broken toys? Buckets of tears? Wastebaskets? Microphones? Newspapers? Ashtrays? Exhibitions? Piles of cabbages stored up for winter?

The key to the whole thing was not Michael's personality. The key was her past life. She didn't feel that her IQ was up to coping with it; even if she tried to work it out on her toes as well as her fingers, she still couldn't get it straight. Michael had left her suddenly, saying she was "too deep." What, me, deep? No one had ever said she was too deep before.

Bloody Londoners.

* * *

I thought my brother hadn't heard me say "Fuck it" when he was burning his stamp collection, but it turned out that he had. He rewarded me with a genuine khaki uniform.

I rolled up the sleeves and the trouser legs, and it still fit me like a tent.

I put on the widest leather belt I could find. It went around my waist twice, and I still had to punch a lot of extra holes in it before I could do up the buckle.

Back straight, chest out.

The basketball shoes fit like pontoons. My feet seemed to stick out miles in front of me.

My pigtails poked out ridiculously, and the cap fell over my eyes.

In the pockets were a bus pass, some cash, a handkerchief, the Little Red Book, and a notepad.

On the breast of the jacket was a Mao badge the size of an alarm clock.

When you do the rebel dance, you need grand gestures – arms akimbo, legs apart, head facing right; you sway dramatically back and forth to the beat of the music.

I went out onto the streets to read the posters and copy them down.

Back home I reported what I'd seen to the grown-ups, but none of them could be bothered with me.

Everywhere I went I hurried.

Puffing and panting.

Full of confidence.

Was I good enough for it now?

Back I went to sign up as a Red Guard.

Shit.

Too late again.

A hero had emerged at our school with a vocabulary of obscenities a hundred times richer than my own. He had written a poster attacking our teacher, which contained two hundred swearwords in the course of its two pages, without a single repetition! The crowds reading the poster blocked the road into the school. The members of the 8–18 Red Guard brigade examined the document through a telescope and concluded that its author was just the kind of tough guy they wanted for the 8–18s.

I never actually found out what his name was, but anyway he was a hero and a tough guy. He stood proudly at the main entrance to the school, basking in the admiration of the crowd, with two long strings of snot dangling out of his nose.

This was too much for me. I was out of there. I honestly couldn't bring myself to admire someone who wouldn't wipe his nose. I just wanted to go home.

I had to walk past him on my way out. Out of the blue he asked me, "Wanna be a fucking Red Guard?"

I was speechless.

"I'm gonna start a brigade of my own so I can be the fucking leader. Catch me brownnosing after the 8-fucking-18s!" He snorted. The string of snot on the left disappeared back up his nose; the right-hand one got longer than ever.

"Yeah . . . okay." I eyed his nose dubiously. He wasn't someone I fancied making revolution with, but the thought of the red armband was awfully tempting.

"Got any money?" He asked straight out, the way the little boys in the school yard used to say, "Got any sweets?"

Anyway I had. I usually did. I pulled out the five yuan I'd brought for my bus pass.

"Hey, not bad!" He took the lot. "We can print up a whole fucking pile of armbands, buy a wad of fucking ID cards, and get a chop cut too. Fan-fucking-tastic!"

"Some of that's for my bus pass. Let me have two yuan for the pass; you can keep the rest."

"Who gives a fucking shit about your lousy pass when there's a revolution on? Go get a couple more yuan from your folks. You can be the fucking 2IC." At last he wiped his nose off on his hand.

"Second in command!" I forgave him the snot.

"Let's go get the chop cut. Tomorrow we'll recruit ourselves a fucking brigade."

Which is how I got my brother's uniform in exchange for a dirty word, and a Red Guard armband and a 2IC cap badge in exchange for five yuan.

Supersnot turned out to be pretty smart. He got hold of everything we needed with the five yuan. He also jimmied open a door in the classroom building and moved in tables, chairs, bookcases, and even beds; then we swept the room and mopped the floor, cleaned the windows and put up a sign calling for volunteers. In a couple of days we had a good-sized brigade. We also recruited a teacher, who asked right away if he could be the political commissar, because he reckoned he could write better than we could.

The political commissar was also a much finer talker than Supersnot. Supersnot's expertise was limited to swearing, but the commissar would talk so earnestly that blobs of spittle would gather at the corners of his mouth and dribble down.

Within two days of its establishment, our brigade had its first assignment: to guard a "landlord's wife" who was to be "deported to her native village."

When it was time for us to take charge of her, we were having lunch at the Divine Harmony Restaurant, so the old ladies in the Revolutionary Rebel Neighborhood Committee and someone from the police station hauled the old woman along to the Divine Harmony to find us. They conferred at some length with Commander Supersnot and the political commissar. Then they made the landlord's wife sit where we could all see her and hurried off to join the queues to buy cabbages for winter storage.

The landlord's wife sat by our table coughing constantly. She took a pot out of her battered basket, lifted the lid, and spat a lump of phlegm into it. That made me think it was phlegm that I was eating. I decided not to look up anymore.

We started to chat.

"Did I ever tell you about when I was going to school and I gave my spare change to an old ragpicker woman?"

"Yeah?"

"It was *her!*"

"Didn't you know she was a landlord?"

"I thought I was doing a good deed, like Lei Feng!"

"She picks up rags. That's working masses."

"Yeah, but she *used* to be a landlord. Like the kind that killed Liu Wenxue."

"It's rough to know who's what. What do you do if you suddenly discover your old man's a landlord?"

"That'd be scary. You'd have to kill yourself!"

"Couldn't you just draw the class line and denounce him? Do you really have to kill yourself?"

"What I want to know is, how do you do it without it hurting?"

"It hurts however you do it."

"What about sleeping pills?"

"I heard they make you want to puke. That's really gross."

"We could look that up somewhere."

"I can ask my mom. She's a doctor."

"What do you want to talk about it for? Got nothing better to do than think about dying?"

"Are we all prepared to die? Yes, we're ready any time . . ." Little Ding giggled as she sang the Youth League chorus.

"This evening . . ." The political commissar pounded on the table and started to make a speech. He had eaten so much there was sweat pouring down his forehead onto his glasses. "This evening there must be people standing guard at all times, and then tomorrow we deliver her to the railway station. During this time we must not allow the class enemy to sabotage our work, and we must maintain our vigilance in case she attempts class revenge or flight!"

Supersnot snorted, "She's so fucking sick she can't run off anywhere, and who's she going to take revenge on anyway?"

The political commissar scowled at him. "Platoon 1, keep watch tonight. Platoon 2, deliver her in the morning!"

"Can the people on duty tonight go home and get their quilts?"

"Get quilts, and don't forget your Little Red Books." The political commissar pushed his glasses back up his nose.

"What good's the Little Red fucking Book?"

"If we haven't got the Little Red Book, how can we unify our thinking, maintain our will to fight, and repel all attacks?" The political commissar became even more earnest, spraying the table with saliva and bits of undigested rice.

He might at least have done it into a jar.

"We must . . . firmly and resolutely . . . safeguard . . . overcome opposition . . . all of them!" The political commissar paused in anticipation of a round of applause. The landlord's wife started choking convulsively. We all watched as with a final splutter she dribbled a mouthful of phlegm into her jar and softly gasped for breath.

"You must behave properly. No talking or doing anything out of turn!" The political commissar admonished the landlord's wife and scowled at Supersnot again. Then he, too, went off to join the queue and buy cabbage for his mom.

The landlord's wife groaned and nodded her head, going on well after the political commissar was out of the restaurant.

"You got a nerve, saying 'Little Red fucking Book!'"

"*I* said that? Did I say 'Little Red fucking Book,' you asshole?" Supersnot slurped soup as he sniffed phlegm. Or it might have been snot he was drinking and soup he was dribbling.

"Y'talktoofingmuch!" Little Ding had a couple of big dumplings stuffed into her mouth. She hadn't said a thing so far, but *now* she did, showering bits of food in all directions.

"What's that?" Everyone watched as she chewed up the remains of the dumplings and gulped them down. When her black teeth finally came into view, she took a deep breath and repeated, "You talk too fucking much." Then she added, "The political commissar got so mad with you that his face was black as a boot brush."

"He's just a stinking fucking intellectual anyway. We can knock him down any time we want."

"To hell with that. We can't knock anyone down. More likely someone else will knock us down!" That was Wazi speaking. After she'd been laughed at for wanting to be an ambassador's wife, she'd gone through a period when her ambition was to drive one of the honey-carts that collected the contents of chamberpots. Then she'd decided to be a ballet dancer and wore practice pumps all the time. Now she'd finished eating; she had taken off her pumps and was packing cotton scraps into the toes so it wouldn't hurt when she walked on her points. No one understood what she was talking about, so no one took her up on it.

Propaganda cars with loudspeakers were driving up and down the streets. Our ears pricked up as they passed and then relaxed, pricked up and relaxed. People walked by.

The landlord's wife was still nodding.

Back home to pick up the quilts.

"If you jump down a well, you choke something awful before you drown." We were keeping watch that evening, still looking for the most painless suicide. The landlord's wife was locked away in a little room across the hall.

"You die pretty much straight after you breathe in the water."

"But if you can swim, you won't breathe water."

"That's scary! You can't die, but you're trapped down there."

"Shit. It's harder than you'd think!"

"Remember when we were in school and they used to tell us all those stories about Party members facing torture? I always used to think if I got caught I'd rather kill myself than be tortured."

"I never understood why they killed themselves."

"'Cause they'd get it even worse if they didn't!"

"Our teacher said they sometimes did it to keep from giving away secrets."

"Better than getting beaten up."

"Still pretty scary, though."

"My mom and the others went to special suicide classes when they were in the Party underground."

"Wish we had that kind of class."

"Why?"

"We keep talking about suicide, but if you actually had to do it and didn't know how, you'd mess up the suicide and land up even deeper in shit."

"How about hanging?"

"That'd be pretty quick, eh?"

"Don't even think about it. The kids in our courtyard used to play at hanging each other. They'd fix the noose just under their chin and then kick the chair away and thrash their legs about as if they were really being hanged. One day one of the kids was playing, and the noose slipped from under his chin to around his neck, so he nearly hanged himself for real. Lucky for him there was a radiator there. He managed to save himself by scrambling over to it."

"The trouble with dying that way is that your eyes bulge and your tongue sticks out, so you look like a spook."

"My granny says you die by choking, so it's bound to be really painful."

"I wouldn't want to look like that anyway."

"Sleeping pills might be best after all."

"But you might puke, remember, and you have to put all those pills in your mouth one after the other. Don't you think that would just get scarier and scarier?"

"It's still the quietest, and you don't look ugly when it's over."

"I think a pistol would be the quickest way – one bang and it's all over."

"But what if you don't aim straight?"

"Let me tell you a fucking story." Supersnot sat on the floor bundled up in his padded coat, his back to the radiator. "There's this guy who breaks some fucking law or other and the judge sentences him to death. But they don't actually execute him; they tell him they're going to bleed him dry. So they get a couple of thugs to put a blindfold over his fucking eyes and then they stick him in the arm with a fucking needle to take the blood out. There's this bucket by him, and he has to listen to the sound of blood flowing through the needle into the bucket. So he just fucking listens: trickle, trickle, trickle – "

"Ugh!" We all groaned. The girls all curled up small in their quilts.

"Don't interrupt!" the boys yelled at us. We'd made a partition of tables in the classroom. The boys lay on exercise mats on one side of the partition, with us on more mats on the other side.

"So he keeps on fucking listening. To start with it's running freely – trickle, trickle, trickle – then slower – drip, drip, drip – as the bucket fills up. His face gets whiter and whiter; he gets colder and fucking colder. Finally the bastard croaks. When he's good and dead, they take another fucking look at the bucket, and it's full of water. No blood at all!"

"So how'd he die?"

"Scared the shit out of him. The magistrate had him blindfolded and made him listen, and the stupid asshole thought it was his own blood! There was some thug pouring water into the bucket, and the needle didn't take any blood at all. You know what that is? Fucking psychology, that's what!"

"Yech!"

"I want to pee, but I don't dare go," Little Ding whimpered.

"Talking of peeing, want to hear the one about the public can?" Someone else was getting started.

"Please, *please,* not now," begged Little Ding.

"If you go to the can, there'll be spooks making funny faces at you!"

"Oh, no!" Little Ding pulled her coat over her head.

"So there's this girl going to the public can . . ."

I needed to go too. I took Little Ding's hand, and we both fled from the classroom as fast as we could so we wouldn't have to listen anymore.

The window of the toilet was open, and cold air was pouring in. The lightbulb was flickering, and as we squatted down I was convinced there was a black hand about to make a grab for us. We talked to each other as loudly as we could manage, and we didn't stay in there a second longer than we had to. We were hitching up our trousers as we left and fastening them as we hurried out of the toilet.

As we went past the room where the landlord's wife was, it was pitch dark and silent. There was a padlock on the outside of the door.

Liu Wenxue was killed by the landlord while he was guarding the commune's — yams, was it? or sweet potatoes? And how did the landlord *do* it?

Another blast of cold air blew after us through the toilet window. It gusted up our trousers and into our bottoms. We shivered as we ran to the classroom and bundled ourselves through the door, leaving the prospect of being murdered outside in the hall.

". . . so all the girls that went to the can were killed and tossed in the cesspit." That story was finished.

"Hear the one about the guy who ate human flesh?" Another was starting.

No one's killing us, so why do we have to talk about eating each other!

"Tell it with the lights out!" As if it wasn't bad enough already!

"No, leave them on!"

"This guy goes out for a midnight stroll, and he wakes up the next morning with his mouth full of blood!"

"I heard that one; he'd been eating a stiff in the night!"

"Do stiffs bleed?"

"Fresh ones do."

"How's it taste?"

"Kind of sour, they say."

"Look over there," I screamed. "There's someone outside the window laughing at us! Help!" Everyone tried to hide under their quilts. Someone flicked the light off.

After staying quiet for a bit, we tried a few more tricks to scare each other, and when nothing would frighten us anymore, we went to sleep.

In the morning there was real blood running into the classroom. When we opened our door, we saw that it was coming from the little room across the hall. Supersnot fumbled for the key and opened the door. The landlord's wife was lying in a pool of blood, gasping for breath. Her throat was slashed, and big bubbles of blood popped out of it each time she gasped. The room stank of blood. The boys called the janitor and told him to get her to the hospital. Blood kept oozing out of her neck. They found a razor blade on the floor. She must have slashed her own throat.

"She almost cut through her windpipe. If she'd done it, it would've been the end of her right there!" said the janitor. "Just kept hacking away with her little slitter."

"Not that easy – putting yourself away," one of the other workers chipped in. "You got to know how it's done. Tough on the old lady, mind, look at all that blood."

So this was suicide. Obviously she hadn't been to classes, which was why she'd only half killed herself. If she'd been to the classes, she'd be away from all this. Now here she was, just a short distance from death, but she had to travel that final stretch gasping through her punctured windpipe, or maybe with the cold air blowing straight in through the gash in her throat. She had to watch the blood oozing out of her or popping up in bubbles. She could smell the stench of it and feel the pain. She was waiting, either for death or for someone to patch her slashed windpipe and sew up her throat while there was still time. No matter whether she lived or died, everyone would call it "suicide to escape justice." She would still be a "pile of dog shit unfit to be called human." When she died, there would be no place to lay her; if she lived . . . if she lived . . . if she lived. . . .

"People who want to die hate you if you save them," said Wazi.

"How do you know?" I asked.

"Read it in a book." She was practicing her ballet positions.

I'd caught a cold.

On the way home, I met my brother at the end of the alley. He sneered at me. "Just go home and stay there. Don't make any trouble." He was wearing polished leather shoes and a khaki trenchcoat. His face was deathly pale. Something was missing – his big, shiny red satin armband, with the Leader's face and the words *Red Guard* embroidered in black.

I hugged my quilt and shivered. My nose was running. I wanted to go to bed.

"I want to be a Red Guard," I protested.

"Piss off." Same as ever.

I shivered. My nose was running. I wanted to go to bed.

When I got to the house, I found that the great red front door that had survived all those dynasties now had a poster pasted on it. On the poster were Mommy and Daddy's names, each character in the names slashed through with a heavy black cross.

4

What kind of man was Daddy? Pale, soft-spoken, not at all like those sleek, well-nourished revolutionary types, always strutting around with their chests out. He was over sixty years old, and he still didn't have a pot belly, which was another thing that made me doubt he was really a revolutionary. Mommy told me that he had run away from home to go to school in the city and had gone on to be a top man in the Communist Party. There were those who felt he was really more suited to being a writer, but when the Red Guards dragged him off, they said that he was actually a landlord. Not a student, not a writer, not a leader, not even fit to be a capitalist roader – just a landlord – the kind of landlord you saw in the cartoons and comic books, scrawny and sly in fur coat and skullcap, exploiting their tenants and squeezing their debtors, bullying the weak but cringing before the powerful!

Whatever he had been, he was gone now, without ever giving me the chance to see what he really looked like, let alone understand what kind of person he was. We ate our breakfast at separate tables that morning, as was our custom. This was a rule that Mommy had made when we were much younger, although whether for reasons of hygiene or for the peace of the grown-ups, I couldn't say. Daddy seldom spoke at table, and he didn't eat much, either. After breakfast he would either go to his office and read or he would chase bugs off the fruit trees. I always felt that he spent more time looking at books and bugs than he did looking at us. Anyway, that day was no different; he looked at bugs and not at me. But I lay on the window seat inside and spied on him through the glass. I thought of all the terrible allegations the posters had made and hoped that I might see something in him that would prove them wrong. Far from finding anything that might refute the accusations, I kept seeing all sorts of reasons for believing he really *was* a landlord. See how pale his face was! How listless his eyes were! How he cared only about fruit trees! How he never did up the collar fastening of his cadre suit!

I went out into the courtyard to get a closer look at him catching bugs. "Ah," he sighed, but he was talking to the bugs.

He said several *ahs,* each time wiping out armies of little aphids with his insect spray.

"Daddy," I asked him, "can you tell me whether that stuff in the posters is true or not?"

"Haha." He wasn't saying my name; it was a laugh. "As to whether you should believe that shit, you will have to study the matter for yourself." He always answered questions indirectly if he could.

"So did that stuff really come from Party Central?"

"Party Central? What bull!" Then he *ah'd* again and blasted another phalanx of aphids into oblivion.

I studied his face. He was unshaven, and a single hair protruded from his nose. As a kid, my favorite game had been clambering up to his neck and tweaking the hairs out of his nose.

"These fruit trees are finished for this year." He was staring at the trees.

It was true then: he *was* a landlord. I stared despondently at the flagstones.

"That clump of bamboo over there is worth looking after. Come Spring Festival next year, we can use some to make palace lanterns." Now he was looking at the bamboo.

That was a special hobby of his, making lanterns of bamboo and paper for the Lantern Festival that follows New Year – that and painting portraits of traditional beauties, both of them the "decadent amusements of the landlord class."

I went inside crying, knowing less than ever what kind of man he was. I'd never really seen that much of him – he would have meetings, entertain, and sleep at the office, and I wouldn't see him at all then. Sometimes when he was strolling in the courtyard I would sneak up behind him and pick money out of his pockets – but after I had the money I'd run away, so I never saw his face, just heard his laugh, "haha." In the evening he would come to kiss me before bed, but all I felt were his bristles. When he held me in his arms, all I saw were the hairs in his nose. He went fishing with my brother and dancing with my mother. When he was writing, his head was bowed. When he was making lanterns, there would be clouds of smoke rising from the pipe between his teeth, so I never got a clear view of him at all. Because of the posters, I suddenly wanted to know about him, but I couldn't find out anything at all. Soon after, the revolutionary rebels came for him, bundled him into a jeep, and took him away.

He never came back. We were told he killed himself.

* * *

The past had carried Huang Haha back, to live it through again. Her head ached, and she felt dizzy. Try as she might, she couldn't stop the flood of memories, nor could she join them together to make a story. The ghosts of her youth came back to haunt her. Her days were spent communing with people from her past, so that she forgot the real world of the present: the present became the past, and she immersed herself in a real world that was gone forever. She lived in the past, keeping to her old ways, as though abandoning them would leave her helpless and naked. Particularly since her arrival in London, she had felt, as she walked the streets clogged with dog shit, that she had suddenly become an example of a Chinese cultural heritage, stretching from Confucius to patent herbal hair restorers, that was both alien to the world in which she now found herself and incompatible with it.

Her mind had become a general store like the ones she had known in the lanes and alleys of her childhood. There the chocolate had lain unsold for so long that it was full of bugs; if you broke open the moon cakes, all the filling inside would be gone, replaced by white fungus and spider webs. It was hard to tell which of the goods were rotten and which were merely shopworn – but it was certain that there were no new goods, and if anything new did come in, there would be no place to put it. So in the end Michael gave as his reason for leaving her, "I'll never understand what's on your mind, and I'll never be able to share it with you." Right now the only thing on her mind was writing her novel, but because this was present tense, she had no idea how she should go about it.

Arguing with herself, Haha stuffed her manuscript into a drawer and went downstairs like a sleepwalker to check the mail. She loved to get letters and to send them. "Why do you write letters all day every day? Can't you face living in the present?" Now that Michael was over the thrill of her exoticism and inscrutability, he had taken to finding fault with her. Sometimes she would get out of bed as soon as they were finished making love and start writing a letter.

"Actually, once I really get down to writing there's nothing worth saying," she told herself. She couldn't talk about the past to the people from her past. They wanted to talk about the present, and the people from her present couldn't bear to hear about the past all the time. So there really was nothing to be said. Her landlord often went off traveling, as did many of her fellow students. On one occasion Haha had applied for a visa to go to Italy, but she had been turned down as soon as the official had seen her Chinese passport.

She tried not to take this kind of thing to heart. When it happened, she merely told herself, "I've been all around China, and there's more of China than there is of the whole of Europe." She'd had a whole bellyful of European literary history, and her grades were better than anyone else's, so what the hell difference would it make if she never went to Italy at all?

"I just can't believe you can't live without one of those." Auntie was always coming out with lines like that. "I just can't believe you can't paint without an artist's pad. . . . I just can't believe you can't learn how to draw even if you don't have a plaster bust." She said it every time Haha came up with some new demand. But for all her protestations, she always found a way to get Haha what she wanted somehow, even in their darkest Cultural Revolution days, when Auntie dipped into her savings to buy Haha the most expensive artist's pad for her sketching. Auntie was certainly a lot easier to get around than the officials at the Italian embassy. Haha had always jeered at Auntie and her "I just can't believes" as a sign of stupidity, but now she saw there was some reason in this stupidity after all — I just can't believe that anyone has to go to Italy!

Whatever she came up against, "I just can't believe" would get her by. When Michael started to talk about what was wrong with China, she could always respond with, "Who cares? England's just a piddling little country anyway, and for that matter so's France."

"I'm beginning to sound like the Auntie of London," she said to herself as she walked out onto the street and felt the cold on her legs. "The chill gets you from the feet up" was what Auntie would say when Haha had tried to get out of wearing her heavy padded trousers. Now Haha dressed more warmly even than the old ladies in London; the girls went out in miniskirts and tights even on the coldest days. At parties, when the Italian girls were giggling and flirting to turn the men on and the French girls were wearing their sexiest fashions, there she would be, earnestly attired in a long woolen dress and high boots. There was a grad student in sociology named Alex, who went on to be a comedian; he told Haha she looked like his mother. An Italian student named Antonia tried to get Haha to dress in one of her miniskirts for a party, but Haha didn't know how to walk in it and wasn't keen on the idea of everyone looking at her legs instead of her face. There was always a party at Antonia's place, full of students from all over the world, a babel of different languages. Almost all the men there were Antonia's past or prospective boyfriends. Men were all crazy about her, but the man she was hot for was Old Gu. To her, he was mysterious and deep. Haha could see that what fascinated her about Old Gu was the illusion that he was all talk and no action. "That's something Chinese men are good at – putting on an act to make women fancy them," Old Gu had told Haha once in one of his disquisitions on sex.

"Can you tell me what it is about him that's so attractive?" Antonia asked Haha.

Because he despises women, she thought. "Because he's so idealistic," she said.

"What do you think he feels about me?"

That you're an airhead, was the answer that occurred to Haha, but she said, "You're his dream."

"Ah . . . if only I could make this beautiful dream go on forever."

"It's a blessing to dream," said Haha. Being one of Old Gu's pals, she could hardly say, "Whoever falls for him is done for."

Antonia kept on going out with a variety of boyfriends and dreaming of Old Gu. But Alex's dream was shattered, or so he told Haha after he came back from a visit to China.

"So what did you expect to find there?" she asked him.

"The revolution. Socialism. But all I found was materialism."

"Why didn't you stay a bit longer? How can you understand a country in such a short time?"

Alex shrugged his shoulders. "I wanted to come home and take baths, go to concerts, eat Indian food."

People always want what isn't there. Haha stood out on the street, still talking to herself.

An old drunk across the street yelled at her, "You women! You're all whores!"

* * *

The political commissar became the head of the revolutionary committee at our school. Supersnot kicked me out of the Red Guards for being a "landlord's brat," but soon after that the political commissar denounced *him* for saying, "Little Red fucking Book," so Supersnot became a "bad element" and was made to write copious self-criticisms and clean the toilets every day. After we had all gone back to school to make revolution, the Red Guard brigades were disbanded and reconstituted by the school authorities as "Little Red Guards." The kids who joined the Little Red Guards were the ones who sucked up to the teachers and wrote testimonies after eating the stinking mess called bitter-memory stew, which people were supposed to have lived on before communist liberation.

I started junior high the year that my brother's class went off to the countryside to become peasants. There was a brigade of goody-goody Little Red Guards there, too, set up by the revolutionary committee. The fathers who had been communist officials had all been slung in jail; the fathers who had been officials under the nationalists were all under protection as allies in the United Front. Little Ding said her father had joined the wrong party; Wazi was mad at her mother for marrying the wrong man; and I said Daddy should have joined the nationalists first and then changed sides, but Auntie said that was all a lot of silly nonsense, because "all our fates lie at heaven's gates." Look at her –

hadn't she done just as badly, she who was descended from the Great Sage?

Later still, Little Ding's mother killed herself, and Wazi's mother followed suit. My mother no longer bragged that "a resolute Communist Party member would never contemplate suicide," but she kept the faith anyway, while Little Ding and Wazi's fathers were out looking for new wives.

"Shit's precious to us farmers," said the team leader, showing us the village latrine. It was our first day in the village as sent-down youths. The latrines were all huts made of plaited straw, with a cesspit behind the size of a swimming pool. When you used the latrine, you had to perch, feet together, and aim backwards over the edge of the pit. If your balance wasn't so good, you risked falling in head over heels. We'd often see dogs, chickens, and pigs floating in there, their corpses surfacing once they'd taken in a bellyful of shit. It was the most revolting death that any of us could imagine – even the most suicidal never considered jumping into a cesspit.

When we got down to work, we learned that shit really was worth its weight in gold. The team leader was a widower of thirty, with thirteen-year-old twin daughters, both of them already promised to soldiers. He was keeping them home to work until they got married, sending them down barefoot into the cesspit for buckets of night soil. Floating on top of the buckets were cocoons, ready to hatch and rattling as the maggots battered their way out. The girls would haul the full buckets out of the pit with a rope and then walk barefoot to the fields, each bearing two buckets balanced on either end of a carrying pole. One time when I passed them, I thought they had been harvesting in the bean patch, because the layer of maggot cocoons at the top of the buckets was so thick it looked like they were carrying beans. In the fields, the peasants would tread the night soil into the squelching dirt as fertilizer, and, sure enough, the crops grew better where more of it was put down. This was why the team leader's house had two latrines.

After the villagers used the latrine, they would simply pull a handful of straw from the wall of the hut to wipe their bottoms and then toss the straw into the pit. As more and more of the straw got pulled off, the walls let light through, and passersby could see that there was someone in there having a shit. When more of the straw was gone, you could tell whether the person inside was a man or a woman. When it was so far gone that all that was left was the frame, the peasants would dismantle it and move it somewhere else, leaving the contents of the cesspit for later use, like money in the bank.

For reasons I could never quite understand, a girl from Hangzhou called Wang Hua agreed to marry the team leader. Her parents had been beaten to death during a Red Guard search of their house, and she had a younger sister still in the city. Wang Hua was able to save money and grain and got someone to take them back home for her sister. Our village was so prosperous that even the pigs ate rice gruel, all thanks to the munificence of those cesspits.

We joked that Wang Hua had fallen for the team leader because of his two latrines. Both of them were a grand size, and, as if that weren't enough, the larger of the two was not a straw hut but a real building of brick and tile. When you went in, you could watch the cesspit glistening in the darkness beneath. It was huge. We would often see the village ducks waddling along in single file, shaking their wings, around the big latrine for a dip in the cesspit. Then, shaking their wings once more, they would return in the same orderly fashion to the pond and jump in. That pond was the only place the villagers had to wash their vegetables, their dishes, and their clothes.

The great advantage of a brick latrine is that you don't have to worry about people watching you while you shit, and this one also had a good solid door on it. From the outside it looked more like a granary. By the hole down to the cesspit the team leader had installed a wooden plank, so you could squat more securely with your feet apart and cut down on the risk of toppling over backwards into the shit.

Because the custom there was to evaluate brides by their poundage, Wang Hua's plumpness made her the choicest young wife in the village. Thus it was only appropriate that she should command the highest bride price. She married the team leader the year after he had married off both his daughters, and so became at a stroke Madam Team Leader and the mistress of an imposing brick house, two latrines, and several grain-fed hogs. The villagers were suitably impressed by the good fortune and prosperity that her pale skin and ample figure portended and offered the opinion that a bride of such corpulence as the team leader's must certainly have cost him a packet. Wang Hua's sister was also brought to the village to attend the county elementary school. For our part we felt that Wang Hua had made a poor bargain, weight or no weight. We all said that with her sort of poundage she could have married a county head. Even if her girth hadn't been taken into account, she could at least have got the local schoolmaster. But there was also a dissenting view: "Does the schoolmaster have two latrines? He doesn't even have *one,* so he has to go shit at other people's places."

Wang Hua was doing just fine, whatever anyone else might think. One day when she and I were headed off to the vegetable patch together, we came on a pile of night soil that had been dumped on a field the previous day and had dried in the sun. Wang Hua said, "If you take the turds and crumble them with your fingers, the vegetables will get all the good of it." Me? Crumble that stuff? With *my* fingers? I stood and watched in disgust as Wang Hua set to work breaking up the turds. Some of the turds were sloppy and yellow inside, and you had to pull them apart. It was like you were handling fresh shit the moment it came out of someone's ass.

"Good stuff, this." Wang Hua was beginning to sound like her old man. Then she casually broke off a leaf of spinach and offered it to me. I took a bite. It smelled of shit, but it tasted fine.

She got pregnant soon after. Then one day she lost her balance in the latrine and fell into the cesspit. The villagers were all agog to see what kind of a shit-headed baby she would have. Actually the child turned out to be very smart and didn't smell bad at all, although he sometimes played with his own turds. Wang Hua subsequently got someone to bring a commode back from Hangzhou and made it a rule of the house that everyone should "pass their motions" at home. She drew a curtain around the commode and would frequently receive the older ladies and young wives of the village and chat with them as she sat and relieved herself. Every morning she would empty the commode out into the latrine, then rinse it in the duck pond, and tip that water into the latrine, too. All this became a subject of some interest in the village. Most people thought it was all rather disgusting, but the village matrons still found a pretext to go around and watch her as she conducted her business from the commode. Some felt this was a style to be followed; others said rude things about her. But none of it made any difference to the ducks, which still made their orderly procession from the pond to the latrine and then back from the latrine to the pond.

* * *

Haha stood confusedly on the street, as past events, people, places, and conversations seeped out through the cracks in her soul and spread over her body like a putrid, furry mold. The ice-cream vendors, the abusive old man, the old ladies taking their constitutionals – all were gone. Her brain was suspended in midair, filled with the memories of putrefaction; below the neck there was nothing, not even a rumbling in her stomach from those indigestible English baked beans.

A little girl came up to her and asked for money.

"You have to let your vital force come out of *here*." Haha was trying to teach Michael *qigong* breathing. His attempts at the exercises made him look like an ape.

"It goes through *here,* comes up to *here,* and then it breaks up *here*. Think it *down,* think it *down*. Did you feel it? Can you feel it now? Can you feel it in your palm?" she asked him.

"No chance," said Michael with a grin. He found the whole thing preposterous.

"*I* felt it." Haha closed her eyes.

"It's all mumbo jumbo."

"You're an idiot."

Haha looked disdainfully at the English book on Taoism on Michael's desk, and at Michael's large collection of books on Asia, and came to a conclusion – he meant well, at least.

Michael had also reached a number of conclusions about Haha. To him she was romantic, matronly, hip, conservative, artistic, unaesthetic, arrogant, obstinate, silly, practical, unrealistic, complicated, austere, serious, sacrificing, inflexible, sexy. But he didn't say any of this – just, "I don't understand you," and so they split up.

"To hell with it. Let's go eat some Chinese food," said Liu Ding to cheer her up.

There were a lot of white people at the restaurant. For Londoners, eating with chopsticks was a symbol of refinement, like eating a bun on a fork in Peking.

Liu Ding gestured dramatically. "Have a good meal, buy some new clothes, and forget him!" She was an operatic soprano from Peking.

"Where'd you get that dress you're wearing now?" Haha asked absentmindedly.

"There was a sale on when I was performing in Amsterdam."

"Will that really make everything better?"

"Sure. When you see how pretty you look in the mirror, it'll all seem fine."

"Have you been performing again recently?"

"Sure. Doing my bit for the motherland, aren't I?"

"How much longer are you going to study here?"

"Who knows? It's ridiculous, really. It's as if my only reason for being alive is to go in for international competitions." Liu Ding had already won quite a few awards, but she was still entered for more.

"Then give it up."

"When I go home, people will judge me by my prizes, not by my music."

"I guess so."

"It's a real treat to be eating Chinese food. How come English food tastes like the crap we had to eat during the famines?"

"It's their idea of being civilized. They have this thing about being natural and eating roughage. Here it's only the uncultured people who eat processed foods."

"Well, screw that! We had enough roughage when we were kids to last us a lifetime. You know those crispbreads they eat? The sight of them makes me want to throw up! We had to eat stuff like that or starve back then, but people here feed it to their guests."

"You must have been hanging out with the big thinkers."

"I'll tell you something else that's even weirder: There was this old woman who was showing off her embroidery, and everyone was telling her how lovely it was. I said it was just the same kind of sewing we did when we did all those embroidered pictures of Chairman Mao in the Cultural Revolution. There's nothing to it! Nobody said anything at the time, but later they told me I'd been rude and the old lady might have taken offense. But that's all her embroidery was! I could do that Mao-picture stuff for a lifetime and not think there was anything to it."

"You want another plate of chicken's feet?"

"Okay. After that I was afraid to go to people's houses. I couldn't just say nothing, but I kept thinking I was saying the wrong thing! Being polite for hours on end really wears you out. It's like being a flunky, only worse."

"You said it."

"Forget Michael. Forgetting's what life's all about."

"How about you?"

"Yeah, that husband of mine – "

"He's your ex now!"

"See? I even forgot I was divorced. That husband of mine – "

"Ex."

"Right, ex. I can't even remember whose fault it was anymore . . . don't know what to do about him . . . maybe I should . . ."

"Uh-uh."

"He said – but he didn't say it . . . that's the way he is . . . except he's not really . . . I never really wanted to . . ."

"Hmm."

"But really . . . *why* . . ." It looked as if Liu Ding was about to burst into tears.

"Michael used to say that he understood me . . . knew what I needed . . ."

"You and he were from different worlds. But my husband and I – we grew up in the same place, and we still . . ."

"'Close together as we are, I'll never know your mind.' Wasn't that in some movie or other?" Haha giggled. "To hell with it all. Just look at yourself in the mirror and forget about him."

"Tomorrow I'm going shopping again!"

"Can we really solve our problems by buying clothes?"

"At least we can make ourselves feel like human beings!"

"Do you ever wonder what it is we're looking for all the time?"

"Companionship."

"Yeah, I suppose you're right."

"Shit. We can't do without it."

"Mm."

"Do you remember when I was in *Madame Butterfly?* That's my favorite!"

"You were great. Perfect for the part."

"That was because I felt in character all the time."

"I'd never have become an opera fan if it weren't for you."

"Which performance did you see me in?"

"It was just before I left China – that would have been eighty-something – at an experimental theater. It was baking hot."

"I remember that! The theater really was hot as hell, and I had to wear five layers of costume! I thought I was going to suffocate."

"Why couldn't you do without a couple of the layers?"

"That was the wardrobe mistress! She absolutely insisted that, if I didn't wear the whole costume, I wouldn't look the part."

"Why do the show in that god-awful place anyway? There weren't even any dressing rooms."

"It was cheap. Opera wasn't popular then, and we had trouble selling tickets. That was the first public performance, just before we took the production overseas, and the company couldn't afford a decent hall. Changing clothes was a real laugh – it was like you turned one way to make up and slip off one of the costumes, and then you turned back and you were on stage."

"You were marvelous, though."

"Every time I sing that role, I'm in tears."

"I cried in the death scene."

"I had an almighty row with my husband after that performance."

"It's not worth it. Why do women waste so much of their time over men? To wreck your life over a bum like Pinkerton! And then we – "

"My husband treats me like dirt. I get so mad."

"Michael says he prefers stupid women."

"I'm finished with him."

"And when men get stupid women, they destroy them. Your Madame Butterfly was so innocent it was amazing."

"My husband and I were at each other's throats the whole time."

"It was like you were really her."

"I ask you – don't you think he took that girl to the opera with him on purpose, just to upset me?"

"Asian women are such dreamers, so submissive and sacrificing."

"So I stamped on the fruit he gave me, and I threw away the flowers, tore up the libretto, and even yelled at his little girlfriend. After that we were well and truly finished. Of course nobody's ever understood him the way I do."

"That bit where you were going to commit suicide was so sad."

"Let's not talk about it anymore. Madame fucking Butterfly."

5

"Rejoice in the release of a Directive from On High!" blared the loudspeakers on the street.

Boom-boom-ba-boom went the drums. Clang-a-lang-a-lang went the cymbals. Ba-boom clang-a-lang!

"Long Live Chairman Mao! Long live long live long live Chairman Mao!" We screamed ourselves hoarse.

It was so bloody wild! So bloody dark! So bloody cold! So bloody late! You could march down the street yelling and screaming with the rest of the rabble, set off firecrackers, shout at the top of your voice, beat drums, hoot with laughter, do voice-training exercises, fart as loud as you wanted – all the things you couldn't do on normal nights. "Long live long live Chairman Mao!"

When we got to where the crowd was thickest, the boys took their chances too, pressing themselves up against the girls and making us squeal with excitement. The whole street was a joyful throng of grown-ups, teenagers, and kids, crowded in and tingling all over.

Everyone waving red banners wanted theirs to be highest; everyone with slogans wanted theirs to be most elegantly written.

It was another big occasion, another mass demonstration. My face glowed with the thrill of it all. I watched, entranced, as the firecrackers shot up to the heavens and exploded. But then –

"That'll teach you, you little bastard!" Someone shot at me with a slingshot. When the pellet hit me, my ear hurt and then went numb, and all the color drained out of the red flags. In all the excitement I'd forgotten: since the day the Red Guards went through the house, I'd become one of the bad-class bastards. There was another of us "bastards" who wanted to go to the toilet and didn't dare for fear that she might draw attention to herself and get beaten up. All she could do was hold in her pee, and when she couldn't manage that anymore, she wet herself. There was a great wet mark down the back of her pants, and more of the pee was running down her leg and onto the ground. When it froze on her leg, she just stood there looking into the streetlights and giggling stupidly.

Our banners were as fine as anyone's.

Crack! Crack! More exploding firecrackers, clanging gongs beating drums shining lights waving banners thronging crowds running feet shouting voices. I was young! I was nimble! I could run with the best of them! I could push and shove! I could shout slogans!

Ping! "Little bastard!" Another pellet hit me.

This time I felt like crying.

Antiphonal choruses of revolutionary anthems welled up from within the crowd. I sang along, and the pain went away.

After the demonstration, the teachers made us stay up all night, the girls embroidering portraits of the Great Leader and the boys writing "declarations of intent" on slogan boards. We were all so fired up that some of us jabbed our fingers right then and there and wrote "declarations in blood."

Our school had been an elite convent school before the Cultural Revolution, but now that entrance exams had been scrapped, everyone just went to the nearest high school. It was a real treat, making it to high school as easily as that. The classrooms were in an old Western-style building with creaking wooden floors and staircases. When you mopped the upstairs floors, the water ran through and rained on the downstairs. When there were people fighting upstairs, it sounded like an earthquake downstairs. All the classroom windows were broken; only in the uppermost and most inaccessible windows did the stained glass still keep out the wind and rain. Blasts of cold air ran obstacle-course races through the building as we sat in class, huddled in our padded shoes, padded jackets, padded trousers, padded coats, and padded gloves, reciting sections from the Little Red Book. Lesson 1 in the English textbook was "Long live Chairman Mao." Lesson 2 was "Long long live Chairman Mao." By the time class was over we all had chilblains.

Because of the new policy of sending everyone to the nearest school, we were all from the same neighborhood, and everyone pretty much knew everyone else. Most of the girls had gingham jackets and patterned satchels, and if anyone appeared in anything slightly different, there would be a chorus of disapproval: "Tut-tut, she's wearing a new dacron jacket, and you can almost see through it!" "Tut-tut, new nylon socks!" "Tut-tut, a gabardine suit!" When boys and girls were put beside each other in class, we always moved our desks a bit apart. Boys and girls never talked to each other, but somehow everyone still knew everyone else's business, and if one person came in with some new bit of gossip, it would be on everyone's lips instantly: So-and-so's father used to be a flapjack peddler, but now he was a respectable worker. So-and-so's family used to have a store until it was nationalized. So-and-so's father was a landlord who was going to be sent back to his village. So-and-so's mother was no better than she should be. . . .

Naturally they weren't too keen on me either.

Portraits of the Great Leader were embroidered with coarse black thread onto a synthetic gauze base. You just followed the pattern on the gauze, sewing crosses onto it to make up the image of the Great Leader. It was easy enough work, and it didn't stop us from chatting and listening to gossip.

Our study group leader steered the conversation around to a girl in our class called Daxiu. She'd been gang-raped when she was still in fifth grade, then she'd been raped by her dad, and now he'd put her out on the streets to earn money for his cigarettes and booze. Her family had only the one large brick bed; the parents would sleep on one side, and she and her customers would take the other. There weren't many families in town that slept on brick beds.

My brother told me that he had read some dirty stuff about "breaching the harbor" in the Ming dynasty writer Ling Mengchu's *Amazing Stories,* but when I asked if I could read the book, he wouldn't let me. Little Ding had said that when men and women got together it was all "kiss, kiss, kiss," but in *The Story of the Stone* there was something called "clouds and rain." Maybe "clouds and rain" was the same as "kiss, kiss, kiss," and both of those were the same as "breaching the harbor."

"She's supposed to have a face mask when she comes to school. It's the uniform, right? Well, she can't afford even that. There was one day I found out that she had only the ribbon but no mask. She'd let the ribbon hang out of her jacket so it would look like she had the whole thing, but I ripped it out so everyone would see the truth." The study group leader was famous for her achievements in daring to wage war on evil people and evil deeds.

One of the girls tut-tutted disapprovingly. "I heard you can always spot a hooligan."

"How do you do it?" someone asked.

"You look at their bums. Hooligans have flabby bums," she smirked.

"Ugh, that's really gross," someone else said.

"You think *that's* bad?" another girl chipped in with a snigger. "The couple next door to us are really nasty. They leave the light on when they do you know what — just asking for all the kids on the street to sneak around and peep in the window." She mimed the children's actions as she told the story.

"That's *really* gross – utterly gross! And you can just bet there are a whole lot of hooligans in our class," the group leader said.

"Like who?"

"I won't name names now. Just think for yourselves." The group leader pursed her lips pointedly, making us all nervous and suspicious of each other. I was afraid someone would find out I was reading *The Story of the Stone.*

"What does it mean, being a hooligan?" one girl asked softly.

"You should examine yourself closely. If there's anything you can't confess, if you can't be open and aboveboard, if you've had improper relations with a man – that all counts." The group leader's voice was menacing.

"Once I was in a train and I was sitting next to a boy all night. We both nodded off and when I woke up, I had my head resting on his shoulder. Does that count as being a hooligan? Have *I* done you know what with a man?"

"Of course you have, and you might have a baby sometime for all I know," said the group leader sarcastically.

The girl gasped in horror. Nobody said another word. We all just worked intently on our embroidery. Maybe all of us had a history of such hooligan behavior, so we were all scared to speak for fear that we would incriminate ourselves and have someone else accuse us of having a flabby bum.

> Off to sweep the graves in springtime
> Sisters twain go out a-walking
>   Kites in hand they go.
>
> Kites above twist hither thither
> Tug on hands the strings a-holding
>   Hurt those fingers so!

Damn your wind, old God in heaven!
Blew so hard the strings a-breaking,
　　Lost my kite! Oh no . . .

Auntie sang merrily.

Was your Auntie really a member of your family?

Auntie always claimed to be descended from Confucius, and Daddy claimed to be descended from the ugly demon Chi You. Auntie really had the same surname as Confucius, but Daddy was a Huang, and who knew whether those were their real names or not? Daddy was almost certainly lying. Chi You was always pictured looking like an ox, and Daddy looked like a goat, so how could they be from the same family? Auntie was a different case. She really had Confucius' teeth, so everyone believed her. She told us that everything the household possessed was always passed on to the eldest son; her branch of the family was so far removed from the line of inheritance that they hadn't even managed to get a taste of the soup from the bones of the leftovers, and all she had got from the Great Sage was the surname Kong. From her great grandfather's time at least, her family had all been agricultural laborers, so she proudly announced to the world that her class was hereditary poor peasant.

Nobody quite knew why it was that Auntie had decided to come to the city. She had gone to her first cousin to ask him to help her find work, and that cousin had contacted his sworn brother, and that sworn brother just happened to be Daddy's mother's second cousin's adopted son. Thus, by creative use of intimate, tenuous, and adoptive relationships, Auntie finished up at our house and was kootchie-kooing at me the moment I opened my eyes. I thought she was my mother, but then I found out she was called Auntie, and later on people asked me whether she was really a member of the family at all.

After Daddy killed himself, Auntie effectively took over as head of the household, and Mommy always deferred to her. The two of them grew more and more alike – it was hard to say which of them changed her appearance more to look like the other, but somehow two completely different people ended up looking like twins.

Mommy was the daughter of a small-time warlord. When she was about eighteen, Grandpa decided out of the blue to hire a foreign-trained tutor for her. Within two months, her head stuffed full of idealistic notions about the French and Russian revolutions, she put on her best satin cheongsam, ran away from their county town, and headed for the communist stronghold of Yan'an. The tutor disappeared at the same time, so Grandpa naturally assumed that he and my mother had eloped; but when he finally met his son-in-law after 1949, it wasn't the tutor at all, it was Daddy, so Grandpa was able to descend to the Springs of Immortality with his heart at ease. He had never liked the tutor. When he heard that the tutor had been blown to bits by a mortar while fighting in the front lines, Grandpa felt just a bit sorry for him, but he was still glad that Mommy hadn't married him. After Mommy arrived in Yan'an with her idealistic notions and her green satin cheongsam, she was put into a drama troupe on the strength of her lustrous eyes. Most of the actresses in the troupe were city girls, expert singers and dancers who also learned to use local dyes to make themselves colored shawls. With these draped over their shoulders, and homemade shoes on their feet, they thought of themselves as latter-day Anna Kareninas. They certainly weren't about to subordinate their femininity to the military lifestyle, and they made sure everyone noticed them. Mommy kept the Anna style all her life – even when she was old and stooped, she would still straighten up, hold out her chest, and look straight ahead at the mention of the name.

"Haha, think of yourself as a peony," she admonished, looking disapprovingly at me.

"More like a thistle." I wiped a dirty mark off my jeans with a blob of saliva.

"Anna . . . ," she tried again.

"I'm not slim enough for that!" I snapped, and walked away.

Mommy's early life had gone by in a dream. She had been an Anna, and her tutor had taught her to say "darling" in English. But after "darling" and "love," it was "bye-bye" and off to the front lines to get blown up, like in some romantic poem, leaving Mommy's English stuck at "darling." Her next "darling," my daddy, was another splendid fellow with an impressive record of death-defying deeds, a less romantic figure than his predecessor, perhaps, but solid and dependable and more mature in his thinking. Thanks to Daddy's high status, Mommy enjoyed privileged treatment from the day she married. No longer was she one of the black-uniformed Annas putting on shows for peasants by the riverside. She had special foods provided for her and got to ride a horse during military maneuvers. When the war was over and they entered Peking, she was the center of attention, with her own driver, bodyguard, and cook.

"Pretty cushy revolution, Mommy," I said.

"Nonsense, child!" Mommy's friends were at pains to set me straight. "All those who joined the revolution fear neither hardship nor death!"

Of course I had to bow to their superior knowledge because they were all VIPs with strong perfume, embroidered blouses, and high-heeled shoes, and who was I to disagree? Mommy was never satisfied with me – if I wasn't too fat for her, then I was too thin, and she was sending me to ballet lessons or dragging me out of bed to do my exercises. Then it was off to the Academy of Dance, where the ballet teacher took out a tape and measured me, first from my neck to the base of my spine and then from there to the soles of my feet. She said that to be a dancer your lower half must be three inches longer than your upper half; in my case it was only two and a half inches longer, and we weren't going to get that extra half inch now, were we? Mommy gave up on ballet and decided I would have to learn to sing opera. I'd been taking voice classes for years and still sounded like a strangled chicken. Finally the teacher said it: "This child's throat is raspy, and she'd be better off not singing anymore." So Mommy made me take up painting instead – anything to keep me from having an easy life and playing skipping games with the other kids after school.

"You could be a success if only you'd make the effort," Mommy grumbled.

I protested, "But my legs aren't long enough, and my throat is raspy." She didn't seem prepared to admit that it might be her fault for giving birth to me with legs half an inch too short.

She drummed her fingers on the table. "Why should you need long legs to be a painter?" she demanded.

"Maybe I'm color-blind," I answered smugly. I hoped more than anything that some doctor would confirm that the child she had brought into the world was a lost cause, so that I could live the rest of my life in peace. But Mommy was absolutely determined that *her* child must make something of herself.

She scowled at me. "We had the doctors do tests on you when you were born, and they told us that you were superior to the other babies in all respects."

"Superior? What's that supposed to mean?"

"Too bad I wasted my time having you!" She looked away from me and sighed.

Wasted *her* time? What was *that* supposed to mean?

But her sufferings in the Cultural Revolution turned her into a real mother. Almost overnight she became an old woman – her hair went grey and hung limply over her forehead. The flesh on her face slackened, and her eyes were sunken in. She squinted at me and didn't drum her fingers on the table anymore. Seeing what she had become made me wish I could do ballet, opera, voice training – *anything* – if only she would be Anna again. But if the old Anna spirit had actually come back, I would still have had to make a run for it.

As for Auntie, everyone agreed that she was the Perfect Woman. In her village they all regarded her as a paragon of propriety, so she was much in demand to help out with marriages and funerals. But she herself never had a man, and I never found out how it was she came to be a Perfect Woman. There's a novel out called *Half of Man Is Woman,* but Auntie got to be perfect all on her own.

"Out of bed now. . . . Eat your breakfast now. . . . Off to kindergarten now. . . . What *did* you do with your hair today? . . . You do the Lotus Dance *this* way. . . . Look at this new dress I made. . . . See the pleats? Spin around and it flares out like a parasol." Auntie used me as her model.

"Auntie, when we spin around at kindergarten to see whose dress flares out most, the boys all lie on the ground and look up our skirts, like this." I showed her.

"Nasty, horrible brats! Just you watch out when you're playing with those boys."

All day we played the exposing-offenders game at kindergarten, and when I came home I dreamed of capturing enemy agents. When I woke the next morning, there were fallen petals on the ground.

"Look how lovely it is in the garden! Why don't we go out, and you can pretend you're Daiyu from *The Story of the Stone,* burying the blossoms." Auntie handed me a little basket, styled my hair to look like a damsel of noble birth, and bundled me out into the courtyard in my new pleated dress to bury the blossoms.

"Blossoms wither, blossoms fall,
Sky can hardly hold them all;
Scent and color fade and flee

. . . what comes next, Auntie?" I was thinking about the movements so much I'd forgotten the words.

" 'Who will pity little me?' "

" 'Who will pity little me' – then what?" I'd been busy with the mincing steps and lost the words again.

"Something about floating, isn't it?" Auntie suggested.

"Oh yes, that's it! Umm . . .

Floating gently on the breeze,
    Springtime blossoms from the trees,
Blowing softly where they may,
    Making silken curtains sway;
Maiden cloistered in her room
    Grieves to see that spring has gone,
Fears to trample to the ground
    Petals that have fluttered down;
Dreads to think what man may come
    And bear her hence, away from home.
Ere another year is done,
    Girl and blossoms will be gone!"

I went through the dance motions and sang whatever lines I could remember from the poem in the novel.

"How can you be through it so soon? You must have got it all wrong, little girl." Auntie swept the petals brusquely into a pile with her big broom.

"Bury them!" she ordered.

"Oh, Auntie, I'm not dressed right." I pointed to my pleated dress. "Why don't you make me a proper opera costume?"

"We won't sing Lin Daiyu again. It's too sad. Next time we'll do Empress Yang Guifei instead." She scooped up the petals and dumped them into the dustbin.

"Was Daiyu Baoyu's girlfriend?"

"That's all stuff from the past, the old society. Little girls shouldn't concern themselves with things like that. Just keep quiet about it when you go out, anyway. Maybe we'd better sing something proper like *The Women Generals of the Yang Family.*"

Auntie had her chest of cut-price treasures, high-heeled shoes, lengths of material, watches, handbags, sweaters, and silk blouses. She would put them on for festivals and for taking me on shopping trips, but even when she was in all her finery, you could tell she was a hereditary poor peasant.

She only read comic books, but she could sing arias from memory, and she really understood opera. She only had to go to a restaurant once and she could reproduce their dishes. One skim through a fashion magazine and she could copy the clothes in it, or even come up with new designs. If Christian Dior had been in China back then, Auntie could have duplicated the Dior collection.

She was proud of her reputation as the Perfect Woman. All her life she adhered to the Confucian maxim "Twixt man and woman, hand should ne'er touch hand." It vexed her that Mommy and Daddy slept together, and she told me that it would be best if I didn't talk to any boys before I was married "unless you're promised to him or I approve." What's that supposed to mean, *promised* to him, *her* approving? If I couldn't talk to any of them, how was I going to promise anything? What damn good was it to me whether she approved or not?

When Yang Fei decided after going with me for ten years that he didn't want to be my husband, I went straight to Auntie and Mommy and told them to find me someone, anyone, that they approved of. I got married then and there and divorced immediately after, which meant that they came to look on me as a piece of cut-price merchandise myself.

Mommy and Auntie grew more and more alike. They would always buy enough material to make a suit for each of them, and you would often see their two roly-poly figures out together dressed identically in black or grey. Sometimes they wore matching linen blouses that went transparent in the sunlight; through one you could see fraying bra straps and sagging breasts, and through the other a pair of virgin's nipples dwarfed by the ample belly beneath. Mommy's room smelled of cigarette smoke and was full of books; Auntie's room smelled of cheap cologne and had a foreign doll that wore jeans one day and a miniskirt the next.

> First year I planted
>   the flowers never came;
> Next year I planted
>   the frost did 'em in;
> Third year I planted
>   the floods were to blame.
> Oh, it's a shame and a sin!

sang Auntie.

"You ought to have a life of your own," Wazi told me.

She was always one for going her own way. First she had dreamed of being an ambassador's wife, wearing clothes like in the kids' movies. Then she wanted to collect night soil and made a point of breathing in deeply whenever a honey-cart went by; later on she was going to be a ballerina and would stuff the ends of her practice pumps full of cotton scraps and work at walking on her points. We went on to different high schools, and, because we lived a long way away from each other, we didn't meet often. Once when she saw me, she slipped me a cat and asked me to hide it at my place for a while as she had heard her building was going to be searched.

The cat's attempts at meowing sounded more like a croak. It also shed hair constantly and pricked up its ears like a dog at the slightest sound. As soon as it got to my place, it jumped onto my lap and refused to get down. Thereafter it got more senile and crotchety by the day, taking perverse pleasure in croaking, shedding hairs, irritating me and being in a bad mood itself, and demanding to be held all the time.

"Useless wretch," I said to it.

It croaked at me and shed a few dozen more hairs on my trousers.

We kept each other company for a year, its hair piling up like the cabbage leaves outside on the street.

Wazi suddenly developed a passion for playing the accordion, but she was accused of playing impure songs, and her school put her in a revolutionary discipline study group whose members had to go along and watch public executions for their education.

The last time I saw the cat was when it jumped off my lap on the day of the big occasion. Later I heard that there had been a dead cat on the street, and someone had tossed it into a dustbin. One of its eyes was dangling down over its nose, and its guts had been ripped out.

It wasn't until several years later, when Wazi's dream of musicianship had been supplanted by who knows how many short-lived passions, that she decided to keep cats again. She took in seven all at once, even inventing a national flag for them. Domestic pets were banned in those days, so the cats were actually illegal residents of the city; they all had to eat, drink, piss, and shit in her one-room apartment, and the place stank to high heaven. When the government finally legalized cat ownership to keep the rat population down, one of Wazi's cats was so excited that he jumped off the balcony and broke a leg.

"You ought to have a life of your own," she urged me over and over again.

I stayed at her place, and the cats kept jumping on and off my stomach all night long. They jumped down from the wardrobe and landed on us as if we were cushions. Wazi ate instant noodles and fed the cats on fish cooked in soy sauce. When I got divorced, she gave me a dog she'd bought on the black market.

I called him Dopey. He was even more an illegal resident than Wazi's cats and would certainly have come to a bad end if anyone had caught him. I tried to get him to shit on a newspaper, because he couldn't go out on the street, but he couldn't be bothered with the paper and insisted on doing it wherever he wanted. Then when he was finished, he would jump on the bed, wiping his dirty bottom on the quilt and covering the bedclothes with shit.

"Off to the bath with you!" I hurled him into the tub. Every time I did this he would shiver and whine pitifully and then slink off and lie beside the stove whimpering.

Dopey ate and slept with me. He didn't actually shit on the bed, but everywhere else was filthy with the stuff. Someone suggested I should take him out just before I went to bed, but the problem was that food just seemed to go straight through him – he was at it all day, from the moment we woke up.

After my divorce, Yang Fei suddenly decided he wanted to come around and talk about the old times. We'd been together ten years, after all. He'd refused to become my husband, pleading devotion to his art, but when he heard I was getting married, he got family urges himself all of a sudden and found himself a suitable wife. Then just before the wedding, he heard that I was getting divorced.

"Why?" he asked.

"Get it over and done with," I told him.

"What should I do?"

"Go ahead and get married."

My saying "get it over and done with" had the effect of starting everything else all over again. Yang Fei decided he would stay the night at my place and be my lover again. But when the time came for bed, Dopey jumped up right on cue.

Yang Fei was frustrated and angry. "Get lost," he yelled.

"Down, Dopey, *down,*" I added.

Dopey jumped onto me and licked my face. Then he looked across at Yang Fei and snarled.

"Dopey! *Get down,*" I ordered as sternly as I could.

Shocked and bewildered, he stared at me.

"Dopey! *Down!*"

So then he started barking at *me.* I picked him up, hauled him out of the room, and slammed the door.

Yang Fei and I lay down together, but we didn't do anything. Dopey lay just outside the door, howling for all he was worth.

And destroyed any inclination I might have had to tell Yang Fei about how I felt.

I opened the door. The dog bounded onto the bed stinking of shit and absolutely refused to get off. If either of us tried to move him, he snarled. Finally he pushed his way in between us, curled up, and started to snore.

"Maybe we'd better just go our own way." In the morning, Yang Fei got up, dressed, kissed me on the forehead, and left. He never came back.

I hugged Dopey and cried, but he just hiccuped.

"He's not healthy," pronounced Wazi when she came around a few days later. The dog was still hiccuping.

"I don't know what's up with him. Do you think he's in shock?" I thought of us shooing him off the bed.

"Poor thing," said Wazi.

Who's the poor thing? I felt like saying. Dopey got a fever a couple of days later, and so did I.

"This is no good; we're both really sick," I told Wazi over the phone. "You have to come over."

"What? He's sick?" Wazi's first concern was for the dog.

"*I'm* sick, too! We've got a fever, and our eyes keep watering."

"Do you think he caught it from you?"

"More like he *gave* it to me."

"Oh, the poor thing!"

Who's the poor thing? I thought again. I wanted some sympathy. "What if we both die?" I asked her.

"Oh, *you* won't die," she laughed.

Sure enough, it was the dog who died a few days later. On the last day of his life we finally managed, through a foreigner who had ways of getting things done, to get Dopey into a hospital. The doctor took one look at the dog and shook his head. He told us the dog was past saving, and it would be cruel to let him hang on any longer. He had a deficiency of the immune system, something like AIDS but not quite the same. At some stage he had also caught canine distemper; then he'd got pneumonia as well and then paralysis, and finally his immune system had broken down completely. The doctor said it wasn't rabies, so I wasn't in any danger if he bit me. I recovered gradually from my own case of canine distemper, thanks to my undamaged immune system and a cold cure from the chemist, but the dog was done for. He had sickened to the point where he was only skin and bone, and he lay around all day, eyes streaming, whimpering and hiccuping.

The doctor said, "This dog hasn't had enough sunshine or fresh air. He should have had more bones to gnaw on. He's been washed too much. He's had a shock, and you brought him in too late."

Wazi glowered at me.

I protested, "But if I'd let him out the dogcatchers would have got him, and when I gave him bones he left bits all over the bed, and if I hadn't washed him so much there would have been shit on the bedclothes all the time, and I couldn't take him to the hospital because he was illegal."

"Do you want to prolong his suffering or let him die peacefully?" the doctor asked.

Wazi started to cry. "You decide," she said.

The doctor sent him to heaven with a needle. I was afraid that, even when he got to heaven, he wouldn't forgive me for throwing him out of the bedroom.

"You've destroyed your own world," said Wazi.

My world? What was that?
Children's songs from the fifties . . .

Flocks of ducks at our brigade,
Take them to the pool to play.
Ducks go quack quack to the pool;
Bye-bye ducks, I'm off to school;
Bye-bye ducks, I'm off to school.

. . . Choruses for Youth Leaguers and Young Pioneers . . .

Our successor generation
Carries on the great tradition,
    Love the people! Love the nation!
Red scarves flutter on our breasts
    Fear no foes! Surmount all tests!
Hard we study, hard we fight,
    Onward! Victory's in sight.
Our successor generation
Carries on the great tradition
Heading on to communism!

. . .

We, the children of New China,
We, the vanguard of the young,
Carry on our forebears' struggle,
Pain and hardship make us strong.
All united as we follow
Our Great Leader Mao Zedong.

. . . Songs for the masses . . .

Our nation's five-star banner red
    flutters in the breeze

As China's sons and daughters sing
   in praise of victories.

. . . Anthems of devotion . . .

On the great highway our regiment goes,
Bold and undaunted, our spirits are high,
Heading the way that the Great Leader shows,
Braving all dangers as forward we fly.

   . . .

The Helmsman leads us o'er the sea,
Sunshine warms the seeds we sow,
Give us the thought of Mao Zedong,
And like the seeds, we grow . . .

. . . Red Guard chants . . .

Take up your pen like a spear in your hand
Summon your forces, attack the Black Band!
Be a path breaker and dare to rebel
   And roll 'em! roll 'em! roll 'em!
   Roll their mother's eggs to hell!

. . . "Quotation songs" from the Little Red Book . . .

Revolution is not a dinner party
   or writing an essay
   or painting a picture, or doing embroidery.
It cannot be so refined,
   so leisurely and gentle,
   so temperate, kind, courteous,
   restrained and magnanimous.
A revolution is an insurrection,
   an act of violence
   by which one class overthrows another.

. . . And political jingles . . .

The Great Proletarian Cultural Revolution
    Is great! Is great! Is oh-so great!

. . . Russian ballads . . .

Ice and snow on the Volga River,
See the horse carts hitched together;
Softly hear the sad song echo;
Hear the carter singing . . .

. . . And the poetry of the Song dynasty patriot Yue Fei . . .

Hair bristles, thrusts my helmet to the skies,
Upon my porch dies down the pattering rain;
Then heavenward I lift my loyal eyes
And shout my fury loud, my heart aflame.

At thirty, gains and glories of the past
Are dust; new battles beckon far away
Stir up your courage, struggle to the last.
Hearts sore from grief, the young men's hair grows grey.

We battle on, determined to atone
Humiliations borne in bygone years;
Our ruler's subjects, weary to the bone
Must suffer still; when may we dry their tears?

Toward the Helan Pass we march afresh
Unto the breach once more our chariots burst.
What joy 'twill be to feast on foeman's flesh
And on their Tartar blood to slake our thirst.

When sacred land once lost is all regained
Home to our sov'reign let us turn again.

. . . Taiwan pop and Mainland ballads . . .

You ask how much I love you,
How much I really love you?

So deep and strong
So firm and true
The moonlight shines my love to you
    Love to you, love to you,
With you is joy, without you pain
When will I be in your arms again?

. . .

Penghu Bay, Penghu Bay,
Granny's home's in Penghu Bay . . .

. . .

Buy my wine, buy my wine,
Everybody come and buy my wine,
Buy my wine, buy my wine...

. . . Parodies of propaganda pop . . .

On the fifteenth day
The moon's light comes
On our heads and up our bums . . .

. . . Chinese and American hits...

Ooh la la la flame flame
You shine on me like flame, flame . . .

. . .

We are the world
We are the children . . .

. . .

Right now I need your loving
Right now give it to me

. . .

Ali Baba Ali Baba
Ali Baba happy little boy

. . .

Koo-koo-ka-choo
Koo-koo-ka-choo
A-oom shoo-be-doo-wa
A-oom shoo-be-doo-wa

. . .

boo-boo boo-boo ba
boo-boo ba boo-boo
boo-boo boo-boo ba-ba
boo-boo boo-boo ba

. . .

I know there is a heaven;
I know there is a hell;
Listen to me people I got a story to tell.

* * *

"Hey! You! I just asked you for some money. Don't you even know I'm here?" The beggar girl was still standing in front of Haha.

Haha never moved.

The girl stared at her for a moment, then turned and walked away.

6

One year one of our friends who had nothing better to do took a trip to Hanyao. There she met a monk who advised her, "You should try to be like the good wife Wang Baochuan." She jokingly brought this advice back to Peking, where she assembled all the information she could lay her hands on about Wang Baochuan. She also set up a Committee to Write New Works on Wang Baochuan, to see how many people there were who could emulate the good wife of history.

She selected that part of the opera libretto where Baochuan has waited eighteen years for her husband Ping, who was forced by his enemies into military service far from home. The participants were required to write versions based on their own lives, using as much of the original text as possible. Inability to use the original would be taken as evidence that the writer's life had strayed from the orthodox and didn't match up to Wang Baochuan's. Those present would all check to see who had been able to use the most of the original text, and that person would be awarded the grand prize – a dog's head sculpted in clay.

The original text read as follows:

> O'er mountain ranges green with tender grass
> Spring wind caresses tips of willow fronds,
> The rising sun spreads bounty on the East
> And darkling clouds are banished from the skies.
> 5   To Wujia slopes I walked to gather herbs,

Before me stood a knight with searching eyes
Who bowed, and "Madam," asked with smiling mien
"Does Wang Baochuan still live at Southern Cave?"
He gazed with eyes that saw me as I am,
10 Shamed by his scrutiny, my face blushed deep.
How like my Ping! But this an officer
Three strands of beard aflutter on his breast.
We talked awhile, 'twas Ping my love indeed
Returned to seek Baochuan in her cold cave.
15 Husband and wife smiled joyful through their tears,
My basket in his hand, he led me home.
No happy auspice warned me of this hour,
He came before my eyes had pricked with tears
Ere magpie called, or lantern flower bloomed.
20 I am a shoot long parched by drought and cold
Brought back to life by sweet, refreshing rain.
My cave was derelict, my bed like ice,
Now springtime sunlight drives the cold away.
Once heaven pressed me down, and earth confined,
25 Now heav'n is high, and earth is mine to roam.
Long years apart, together once again,
We talked of times gone by, confirmed our love
'Til lamp oil all was spent and moon had gone,
The fifth watch sounding told us day had dawned.
He told of
30 Injustice borne through eighteen bitter years,
His loss of status, long and cruel campaigns.
But now, as knight and nobleman enfeoffed,
Our sov'reign orders his return to court.
Making me
Joyful one instant, furious the next,
35 Fraught now with anxious fears, now laughing free,
Emotions mixed, conflicting, hard to bear.
Commander Mu dealt graciously with Ping,
The monster Wei's cruel treatment rankles still,
That grace and venom both will be repaid,

40 This day my Ping reports them to the throne.
Now flowers bloom again, our smiles return,
For eighteen years we languished in the cold
Since Ping went East to fight the bandit hordes
And left me sorely lacking clothes and food.
45 The monster Wei spread calumnies and lies,
My military pension was denied.
Yet Baochuan ne'er by hardship was cast down,
With these two hands I labored night and day,
My neighbors succored me in times of need,
50 State charity I neither took nor sought,
And thus survived as year succeeded year
Awaiting Ping's return to our cold cave.
That blackguard Wei once strove to harm my Ping,
Whate'er he suffers now is well deserved.
55 My father bade me take another man,
But Ping returned in honor to our home,
Baochuan his wife is pure and undefiled.
Skies clear, sun shines, all nature is in bliss,
Hardship is at an end and joy is here.
60 On this my father's birthday, to our home
Come officers and courtiers, friends and kin,
Among them surely comes the demon Wei
How will that chancellor regard me now?

The one most likely to win the dog's head was Mingjuan:
it was almost as if the libretto had been composed with her
in mind. With scarcely a pause for thought she dashed off
her version:

O'er mountain ranges green with tender grass
Spring wind caresses tips of willow fronds,
The rising sun spreads bounty on the East
And darkling clouds are banished from the skies.
5 I heard somebody knocking at my door,
A foreign man it was *with searching eyes*
Who greeted me and *asked with smiling mien*

Mingjuan, my dearest love, have you been well?
He gazed with eyes that saw me as I am,
10 *Shamed by his scrutiny, my face blushed deep.*
How like my love! *But this* in Western suit,
Long hair and sideburns gave a look of youth.
'Twas he, disguised as overseas Chinese,
Returned from distant lands me to surprise,
15 *Husband and wife smiled joyful through their tears,*
To show me his true face he doffed his wig.
No happy auspice warned me of this hour,
He came before my eyes had pricked with tears
Ere magpie called or dream had let me know.
20 *I am a shoot long parched by drought and cold,*
Brought back to life by sweet, refreshing rain.
My bed like ice, forlorn as wintry caves,
Now springtime sunlight drives the cold away.
Wind blew *me down,* my road *confined* and small,
25 *Now* winds subside, *and* roads are *mine to roam.*
Long years apart, together once again,
We talked of times gone by, confirmed our love,
For hours we talked, until the *moon had gone,*
The fifth watch sounding told us day had dawned.
Look back on
30 *Injustice borne through* ten long *bitter years,*
He in his cell, yet our love constant still,
Released from jail, to college he was bound
Then overseas, to study far from home.
Our life is
Joyful one moment, *furious the next,*
35 *Fraught now with anxious fears, then laughing free,*
Emotions mixed, conflicting, hard to bear.

[At this point, Mingjuan briefly allows herself a freer hand.]

Divided from each other half our lives,
Our little daughter did not know her sire.
Our fate was like a skiff upon the sea,

40　Upon great waves by savage tempests borne,
　　Now riding high, then suddenly cast down.
　　No matter now what perils lie in wait
　　I nothing fear, but work with might and main,
　　Now flowers bloom again, our smiles return,
45　We cast our minds back over ten long years
　　Truly we had our fill of grief and pain.

[Now her version comes back to the original.]

　　Yet Mingjuan *ne'er by hardship was cast down,*
　　With these two hands I labored night and day,
　　My neighbors succored me in times of need,
50　My parents' *charity* I gladly *took,*
　　And thus survived as year succeeded year
　　Until my husband's star should rise again.
　　The Gang of Four *once strove to harm my* love,
　　Whate'er they *suffer now is well deserved*
55　My bosses *bade me* draw dividing lines,
　　But he *returned in honor to our home.*
　　Mingjuan *his wife is pure and undefiled.*
　　Skies clear, sun shines, all nature is in bliss,
　　Hardship is at an end and joy is here.
60　Now we are here together, pens in hand,
　　Adapting this libretto to our lives,
　　Committee members with your dog's head prize,
　　How will you worthies all *regard me now?*

All present gasped in admiration. She had kept to the original in all significant respects, and, but for the creative flourish of lines 37–46, she might even have passed for a latter-day Wang Baochuan! We looked first at the passages marked as identical and then at Mingjuan. She blushed crimson and turned away to hug her daughter.

"Not much doubt about it," said the committee chairman. "The dog's head's as good as hers. Is anyone prepared to challenge her for the honor?"

"I give up," said Wazi. "My life's been too far from Wang Baochuan's to give me any chance."

"I doubt that I'll get the prize, but I just did it for fun anyway. Now it's written, we might as well see how much I miss the dog's head by." Little Jiang handed over her draft:

> O'er mountain ranges green with tender grass
> Spring wind caresses tips of willow fronds
> The rising sun spreads bounty on the East,
> And darkling clouds are banished from the skies.
> 5 He's meeting me tomorrow; we'll embrace,
> When I get off the plane in Canada,
> And we shall see how well we get along,
> He'll ask me what I've done these many years.
> He'll *gaze with eyes that know me as I am,*
> 10 But there's no way he'll see *my face blush deep.*
> I know how much we've aged these last two years,
> Our faces troubled, white hairs on our brows.
> I'll ask again of problems unresolved,
> I go to him to give us one more try,
> 15 I'll force myself to *smile* despite my *tears,*
> For once upon each other we relied.
> No preparations have I for *this hour,*
> No pricking eyes, no letters, not a word,
> As anxiously I await tomorrow's dawn.
> 20 *I am a shoot long parched by drought and cold,*
> When will I know that *sweet, refreshing rain?*
> My life is colder than a *derelict cave,*
> And even if the *springtime sunlight* shines
> I know that *heav'n* will *press,* and *earth confine,*
> 25 Who knows if I'll be free the *earth* to *roam?*
> 'Tis said when wives and husbands speak *again*
> Though parted long, they *talk of times gone by,*
> But he in letters sent and phone calls home
> Expressed no interest to know my heart.
> *He* only

30 Complained, expressed resentment at his life,
Unloved, uncared for, unadmired, alone,
Untutored in the language of the land,
In drunken haze resigned to pass his days.
Making me
Angry one *instant, furious the next,*
35 *Fraught now with anxious fears,* no smiles for me,
Emotions mixed, conflicting, hard to bear.
A *gracious* cousin helped him overseas,
That he should hit the bottle *rankles still,*
My worrying for him has worn me down,
40 Soon I shall find if it was worth my while.
Now, visa tightly held, my *smiles return,*
The last decade a sick shambolic dream
Since he lost hope and drowned his grief each day,
Who knows how much I went through these ten years?
45 Each day he'd stagger home and then collapse,
Talk drunken nonsense, all his senses gone.
How many times I thought we should divorce,
But for our former love, I sadly stayed.
Still his behavior worsened day by day,
50 Spending his nights somewhere away from home,
Resenting me, his sober, normal wife,
And finding joy in other women's arms.
After he left, I found more peace in life,
My good friends *succored me in times of need.*
55 There are more men than this one in the world,
I should seek happiness for my own sake,
But still I can't forget the love we knew,
And wish I might rekindle it once more.
I need no *honor* from him for *our home,*
60 I do not need him *pure and undefiled,*
Only that both of us should truly care,
And that he be concerned to know my heart.
Now our sorority is met today,
Old friends come here from every walk of life,

65   Adapting this libretto to my tale
     I ask my sisters, What am I to do?

"If this wasn't a committee to select a Wang Baochuan, we'd be certain to award you the dog's head," said the chairman.

"You were way off," Wazi complained. "Even when you used the same words as the original, the meaning was different." Then to console Little Jiang, she added, "Mind you, if it was me writing it, I wouldn't be as much adapting the original as destroying it."

"Okay, okay! Dog's head or no dog's head, I can't stay here all day. I might as well leave you with mine for a laugh." Little Ding tossed a sheaf of papers down.

Everyone gathered to read her version:

Grass, tender, withered, dry, it's all just grass,
All sorts of wind can blow the *willow fronds.*

[After reading this far, we all looked at Little Ding. Mingjuan's little girl said, "I just knew Auntie Ding was going to be best!"]

The sun goes down, of course the moon comes up,
The *clouds* have no effect on joy or grief.
5   I went to disco at the Sheraton,
A man came up and asked to dance with me
A calculating smile upon his face,
He said, "You sure know how to move it, babe."
He gazed with eyes that saw me as I am
10 And lingered lustful on my shoulders bare,
It was my ex, a man of rank and power,
Whom I had left so I could find my way.
I look back at sweet dreams of years gone by:
I was eighteen when I moved in with him.
15 Sex under age could get you jailed back then,
But running risks just added spice to love.
Whenever I told friends of our affair

It shocked them when they knew what I had done.
But all my dreams were of domestic bliss,
20 A life of children, laundry, kitchen chores.
That flirting with the boys was just for fun,
My heart was set upon a husband true,
And I was lovely in my wedding gown.
How could I know that marriage was a bore?
25 My childhood friends still came in search of me
To take me off to parties every day.
While hubby busied making his career
My friends got drunk and lay around the halls,
That narrow-minded husband thought me loose,
30 Kicked out the boys and ordered me obey;
One great big row, and then we got divorced.
From that point on, no worry and no stress.
My marriage *pressed me down,* I was *confined,*
Divorced, I'm *high* on life and free to *roam.*
35 The fuddy-duddies sneered and slandered me,
Said I had gone against their "normal" way,
They scorned my excellence at work and school.
When I wore pretty clothes, they called me slut,
They made me angry and I spoke harsh words,
35 Knowing they'd not respect me anyway.
Through friends I bought myself designer clothes,
My low-cut dresses made the men take note.
Let women do whatever women please
Not hide in clothes that cover neck to toe.
40 I'm young and free; I'll choose the road I take
What right have you to ogle or to sneer?
Stark naked, drunk, I stand before the glass
I know that pain and sweetness take their turn.
You say a girl should always know her place,
45 But I will flirt and kiss what man I choose.
You say that Chinese women are demure,
But I will show my cleavage to the world.

You say I should be prim and strive to please,
But you delude yourself with fantasies.
50 And I despise you! I will break away,
Now I am free of care, *and smiles return,*
You worry about *honor* for *your home,*
You're welcome to be *pure and undefiled.*
Heaven and hell will both be full by now
55 Primordial chaos sure is long since stilled.
My body's mine, you're yours and she is hers
In our own bodies we will live our lives,
And when those lives are done we'll wind up dead,
We might as well have fun along the way.
60 Good luck will follow grief in its good time.
When fortune's time is up, disaster comes,
Disaster, fortune are each other's twin.
We choose which road we take, have just one try.
Today we're all obsessed with being pure
65 Tomorrow every woman for herself,
But when time's up, bye-bye, and off you go.
Ho-ho-ho, off you go,
The world's in chaos, don't you know.

Mingjuan was the first to speak. "Compared to you, I've hardly lived."

Little Jiang grimaced at her. "What are you complaining about? You've won the dog's head, haven't you? You've lived the moral life; it's deviants like us that have hardly lived."

"What does it matter who's moral or deviant? A life's a life after all," someone said.

"Maybe we've really lived; maybe we've hardly lived. No two of us have been the same. Even Mingjuan hasn't been exactly like Wang Baochuan."

"Sure. Either you live life by the libretto or you follow some other book."

"But the libretto was written by someone, wasn't it? It's all in the way it's written. And then everyone passes absurd judgments on it, believing whatever they say is right must be right."

"Who was it came up with Wang Baochuan? She's supposed to have made all her decisions by rolling the dice, but we can't do that, can we?"

"That's how people used to run their lives. You had a lot to put up with being a wife back then."

"Hell, is there no way we can get an easy life?"

"There's no way."

"How can we live right?"

"Anyhow is just fine!"

"How are we . . . ?"

"What the hell! Here we are, a bunch of old women with the best part of our lives behind us, and we're still hung up on questions of right and wrong, worrying ourselves silly about time and morality. If you want to know how to live, you'd be better to ask the little girl!"

As the discussion wound to a close, everyone turned to look at Mingjuan's daughter.

"I'll tell you a secret if you promise not to tell anyone else." The little girl whispered behind a raised hand, "My daddy has a lover."

* * *

The postman arrived and stuffed the mail through the letter box. As he was turning to go, he noticed Haha standing motionless in the street and was about to give her the customary "'Morning." But then he saw that she had not even glanced at him and gave up on the idea. "Funny people, these Asians," he mused.

The pavement under Haha's feet vibrated from the postman's step, so slightly that only small animals and Asians could sense it. The shock brought her body back in contact with her mind. She turned back to the door to pick up her mail. Letters were her world, or as Michael put it, her contraceptive device, because when she was reading or writing a letter, she was too absorbed for anything else.

Clasping her mail, she padded upstairs.

7

Dear Haha,

That story I wrote about my cats has landed
me in all sorts of trouble. Now my cats have become
celebrities; there are all these reporters who keep coming around and asking me how they are. And then there
are people who write tirades about the degenerate life-
styles of artists, giving me and my cats as a prime case. I
tried taking the cats to my father's place, but they all
got colds and stomach ulcers. There's a big one I call
Prince who's taken to sneering at me as if I'd done
something terrible to him. . . . I bought a mouth organ
so I can play to them when I'm not busy. . . . When cats
go crazy, they're crazier than people are . . .

How are you these days?

It's so hot here. . . .

Wazi

From the day Little Ding and I shouted "your mother's
cunt" in the school yard, we became the best of friends. One
day I told her, "Our house was searched by the Red
Guards!"

"Fantastic! Great! Ours was searched too!" Her eyes widened with delight.

"My mom and dad's salaries were cut off. They're down
to living expenses!"

"Same with mine!"

"My mom and dad got locked up!"

"Mine, too! My dad's in jail, and it's a jail that was built on his orders, for locking up nationalist officers!"

"Amazing how things change, eh? Like in a book." This was a real thrill.

"You remember what it used to say in the stories about 'united in disaster at opposite ends of the earth'? Who'd ever have thought that it would apply to us?"

"Yeah, right. And what about 'pitiful victims of the same fate'?"

"Right! We're what they call 'friends in need.'"

"Yeah! We'll have to 'make a sacred vow.'"

". . . A 'Peach Garden Oath.'"

"'Even under threat of death . . .'"

". . . 'I'd never let you down.'"

"'Hook our fingers tight together . . .'"

". . . 'Be best friends for ever and ever!'"

From that moment on we became friends who had hooked fingers in undying loyalty. Later on we also hooked fingers with Wazi.

"We get the bits by the ears clean; then we rinse around the back of the head." That was what Auntie always used to say to me when she was washing my hair. Now I thought of her words as I did the same for Little Ding.

"Okay, it's done." I toweled her hair dry. She hadn't washed her hair since her mother was arrested.

"How's it look? It feels great!" Little Ding was beaming as she combed her hair.

"Hold on! Let me look!" I suddenly realized something was wrong.

"What's up?"

"Oh, hell!" I wailed. "I've screwed up!" I started to laugh.

She rubbed her head and looked at me as if I was crazy.

I was laughing so hard I could hardly speak. "I did the bits by the ears," I spluttered. "Then I rinsed around the back, but I forgot all about the top of your head. Now there's shampoo in it as well as dandruff. It's worse than ever!"

"What the hell. I'll just comb it a bit harder." Little Ding hauled her comb through the tangles.

"Let's go to the bathhouse down the street. You ever been?"

"No. There's nobody to keep the boiler going at our place now, so I can't wash."

"Silly! Come to the bathhouse with me. It's really fun."

So I took her along to the public bathhouse, where we talked and shrieked and giggled and scrubbed each other's backs.

"It's great. We'll have to come here again. It's much more fun than washing at home." She was watching all the naked women wandering about.

"Do your tits itch?" she asked me.

"Mm." I was embarrassed to admit it.

"Mine too. It's scary, like you can feel them growing. Sooner or later they'll get all big and floppy like those old girls." She stole a look at the women around us.

When we got back to my place, we searched out a couple of my mother's bras and tried them on. They slipped off the minute we moved. If we lifted our arms, they ended up around our necks. We almost died laughing.

"Did you ever eat cabbage rolls, Little Ding? Come and try. There's one each." Auntie gave us each a cabbage roll coated in cornmeal. We'd been living on an allowance from the revolutionary rebels since Mommy and Daddy's salaries were cut off, and cornmeal was cheaper than refined flour.

"Smells great! Better than a four-course dinner," said Little Ding.

"My appetite's much better now. Auntie makes flat cakes and cabbage rolls for me every day, and there's a kind of pickle that's just yummy – really, it's better than meat," I mumbled through a mouth stuffed with cabbage.

Little Ding sat on the bed and crossed her legs. "Seems like your place is much cozier these days."

"Sure. That's 'cause it's smaller. It was so big before it was spooky. Now that we've got the bed here as soon as you come in it's much more comfy," I said contentedly.

"Did they seal up all your other rooms?" She looked out across the courtyard.

"Yeah, they did, and it's better that way. Saves us all sorts of trouble. Now we eat and sleep in the same room, and we don't have to move around."

"I don't see why they didn't seal up our house, too. Maybe I should do it myself, so I won't get nervous about all those rooms. Then I can move a table and a bed into the dining room and close up all the other rooms. That'd be great." She made her decision: "If they won't seal up the rest of the house, then I will."

A couple of days later she heard about her mother's death, and I heard about my father. We wept together for a while; then Wazi had us around for a feast of dumplings, and that made us feel better. It occurred to Little Ding that she was now free to do whatever she wanted. Shortly after that, Wazi heard that her mother had also committed suicide. After spending two months in tears, she announced that she too was now free.

One day after we started high school, Little Ding dashed around to see me in a state of great excitement. I was holding the cat Wazi had given me, the one that shed hair all day.

"Guess what's happened to me," she gasped. Without waiting for me to say anything, she blurted out, "Got a boy-friend!"

"Ooh-eee! A boyfriend! Is it fun?" I forgot the cat.

"You remember the song we used to sing in primary school that went, 'There's a man I love, and he's by my side'? I always used to think how wonderful it would be if it actually happened. *So,* there I was walking down the street, and this *boy* comes over to me and asks, 'What school are you in? What's your name? Want to go out with me?' So I went out with him. You know how all the boys talk about 'getting off with an old lady'? Well, that's what it's all about. He's 'got off' with me, and I'm his 'old lady'! We made a date to go to the park together, and we sat on a bench in the evening just like in all those love songs. *Then* he leaned over and kissed me! On the cheek first, then on the mouth. Scared the life out of me. But when he did it, ooh, it was so exciting, just like you read about! We stayed in the park kissing until it got dark. He was hugging me so tight!"

"Ooh!" I didn't know what to say. I just curled up on the bed and gaped at her.

"I'm so bloody happy! We're going to the park again tomorrow." She started to sing loudly.

"Fantastic!" I stamped my feet in excitement. The cat croaked at the thrill of it all.

We celebrated her good fortune for the rest of the afternoon; then off she went.

She was back a couple of days later. She didn't mention it, so I just had to ask her, "Well? What was it like? Was it fun?"

"I don't know. I just lost the urge somehow. All he wanted to do was kiss. As if there wasn't anything else in the world to do! If that's all there is to being in love, I don't think I'll bother. I'm going to break with him."

"Oh, no!" I groaned with disappointment.

"You know what I decided I'm going to do?" she said smugly. "Read. I've discovered that reading is the most fun there is. I've started to read through all the books on Daddy's shelves, so I won't have any time for going out with boys." She picked a slice of toasted bun off the grill and crunched it.

I put my chilblained hands closer to the stove. The cat

stretched lazily in my lap and then got down to beg some toast from Little Ding.

In a couple of years Little Ding had read the masterworks of Chinese fiction, not to mention Shakespeare, Tolstoy, and the collected works of Marx, Engels, Lenin, and Stalin. She started to smoke, and I started to paint.

"It's no use!" I said.

"What's wrong?"

"I don't have a model. My teacher told me I have to have a model to do the human figure."

"What's the problem? There's people everywhere."

"Just anyone won't do. I need someone to pose nude, and I can't find anyone. Apparently there was some artist who got arrested for hiring a nude model on the quiet."

"What are you going to do?"

"I don't know. Maybe I'll just give it up. If I'm never going to do figures I can't be a great painter." I was almost in tears.

"Okay then, I'll sacrifice myself for art. You can paint me." She stripped off her clothes and lay on the couch naked, her arms over her face.

When my teacher saw my first figure study, he said the torso and buttocks were out of proportion.

"*What* did he say?" she asked. We were looking at the painting.

"He said the proportions of the torso and buttocks were off."

"Well, I can't do anything for you now your teacher knows what I look like naked."

"But he doesn't know who you are."

"I still don't ever want to meet him."

"You won't meet him. I'm never going to see him again either."

"Why's that?"

"His girlfriend got picked up by some kind of a talent

scout, and he's so mad he says he's never going to have anything to do with women again."

"Is that right? Just because the guy picked her out, it doesn't have to mean she's going to end up as someone's concubine, does it?"

"The problem is that her family is convinced they've got it made from here on in, so they've told her to break off with my teacher."

"What's your teacher look like?"

"Ooh, he's really neat."

"I've just been reading this book that's really scary. You have to read it when I'm finished."

"What's it called?"

"*The Golden Lotus.* Ever heard of it? When you read it, you'll know all the things men and women do when they do you-know-what. When I think of my parents doing it, ugh, it's revolting! That's the way we got made."

"How do you mean, 'got made'?"

"Just read it, and then you'll know."

I started reading *The Golden Lotus,* but before I'd got to what you-know-what was all about, Little Ding made another of her quantum leaps.

When I went around to see her one morning, she opened the door in her bra and panties and then bounded back to the bed, where she lay with her eyes closed, directing passionate kisses into the air.

"Ahh." She opened her eyes a crack. "Ecstasy!"

"What's up with you this time?"

"I've got a man, and he stayed here last night!"

"Did you – ?" I couldn't bring myself to say it, but images of *The Golden Lotus* flashed through my mind.

"Sure we did. Love isn't just kissing you know; love is two people coming together. Now I understand what my parents did. It's not wicked at all, not like in *The Golden Lotus.* It's sublime – I tell you, sublime!"

"Ooh!"

"You bleed the first time, and I bled lots. I was really scared, and it hurt, too, but it makes both of you feel really wonderful."

"Ooh!"

"That's what love is all about. I'm going to marry him!"

"You're *what?*"

"Well we're going to move in together anyway. I'm paying my respects to the in-laws tomorrow." She bounced up and down in excitement.

I felt a bit resentful. "I'm sorry you're not going to be one of us anymore."

"Don't get upset. You'll have a boyfriend yourself soon enough, and if we add a few boys to our group, we'll have an even better time, won't we?"

Two years later I met the painter Yang Fei. First we painted together, and later he said he loved me. So that's how I learned about love and caught up with Little Ding, although Yang Fei was always the romantic lover who refused to become a husband. When Little Ding's boyfriend's father was let out of jail after the Cultural Revolution, he gave his consent to their marriage. By that time they had been living together for seven years. In their eighth year they divorced, and in the tenth year Little Ding hit the bottle.

"Haha," she yelled up the stairs.

"C'mon up!" I was afraid she would disturb everyone in the building, yelling like that. We'd all been moved into apartment buildings by then, and if you raised your voice in the courtyard, you might as well be announcing your personal affairs to the entire compound.

"Every bloody thing's gone wrong today. I'll come up if you've got anything to drink; if not, then screw it, the boys are waiting for me anyway." She was still yelling.

"You can come up. I've got whatever you want." Anything to shut her up.

"Fuck it all! I had a fight with the bosses at work this

morning." She took off her jacket as she came in. "Where's the booze?"

"Okay, okay, it's right here," I said hastily.

"Oh, great." She poured herself a glass and drank it off and then stripped off some more of her clothes. "What do you think of my figure? The boys all say I'm gorgeous." She was down to her bra and panties and was admiring herself in the mirror.

I thought of the day ten years before when she'd been my model. She certainly hadn't been as gorgeous then.

"You look fabulous." I really meant it. "You've got a body like an athlete."

"Just because I'm fucking divorced, the bosses think I'm a piece of shit. I'm the best they've got, but they still put me down, the assholes!"

"Don't let them get you down. You are who you are!"

"Sure. Cheers!"

"Cheers!"

"Screw the fucking bastards!" Her swearing had come a long way since we worked out together in the school yard ten years before.

"That's the way it is here, right?"

"The hell with them. I'll go with whatever fucking man I want!"

"Damn right!"

"I like the innocent ones better these days. The old bastards just want to use you!"

"I don't know. I like them older."

"What the hell! Old and young, there's something to be said for both. What was it Isadora Duncan said? That men are like instruments?"

"Like songs."

"Yeah, songs. A different tune to each, right? Well I'm not just going to sing one fucking tune!"

I laughed.

"Now I feel better. Best way to cheer up is to talk to old friends. How are you and Yang Fei doing these days?"

"Oh God, I'll never figure him out. He keeps telling me how much he loves me, but he won't get married."

"What's so bad about that?"

"I want marriage. I want security. I want a husband."

"You're an idiot."

"All very well for you to say. You've been married; you know the taste of it."

"What d'you mean, *taste?* Ever tasted gasoline?"

"Forget it! I want a real home, whatever you say. And I don't want to waste my life."

"You're telling me I waste my life?"

"I'm just saying we don't all want the same thing."

"You think you're so superior, don't you?"

"I'm not you. That's all."

"Yeah, you're Miss Chastity, and I'm a tramp! You're living a dream, and I'm in the gutter!"

"I never said that, but you can't make fun of me for having dreams."

"I didn't mean to make fun of you. I wish you well. I'm going. I don't want to keep the boys waiting too long." She started to get dressed again.

"Take care of yourself."

"Don't get me wrong. You needn't think everyone who doesn't dream lives in the gutter." Then a parting shot as she was leaving: "At least the boys I go with aren't all hypocrites!"

"Dreamers aren't all hypocrites, either!"

"Bye," came her voice from down the stairs. Then: "Hey! Haha!"

"What now?"

"I didn't bring any rubbers with me tonight. You got any to spare?" In a voice loud enough for the whole compound to hear every word.

Xiaobo opened a psychological counseling service, charging twenty yuan per hour. I went to consult him about my breaking up with Yang Fei.

"You're expecting too much," was his conclusion on my case. "Nowadays people all want too much."

"All I want is a home and a husband. What's so unusual about that?"

"That's a lot to ask."

"Why? Everyone else has it."

"Don't you know what kind of man he is? He's an *artist.*"

"I hate that word."

"But you love the man, don't you? Settle for that. You know he loves you too."

"That's all there is to it? Love's supposed to be about giving, and he can't even be bothered to be a husband."

"That's because he's a modern man. I keep telling you, and you don't seem to understand: modern men have things on their minds. Why else would I be in the counseling business? Who cares whether you're married or not these days? You love each other; you're together, and that's enough. You have to admit you wouldn't be happy without him."

"If he doesn't want to get married, I'm not going to beg him. We'll see who's happy!"

"You're not being reasonable. Who ever said there was equality in love?"

"How can it be love if he doesn't want us to share our lives?"

"Does love have to be so serious? It's only love!"

"Just you wait! I'll find someone else!"

"We'll see."

"Is my time up? How about the twenty yuan?"

"We're buddies. This one's on the house. Actually I feel like I need some counseling myself. All I want to tell you is this: don't take advice from people like me. Just do what you want, don't do what you don't want, okay?"

Dearest Haha,

   I miss you so much . . .

   There's something I need to discuss with you. Someone's arranging marriages for Auntie and me. One of the men is a war veteran, and the other is a scholar who studied abroad. The old soldier wants me and the other one wants Auntie. Does that sound odd to you? Everyone here seems to think the matchmaker got us paired the wrong way around. . . .

   Auntie and I want your opinion because you understand these things more than we do. Your brother's dead set against it and says the family's going down the drain. . . .

   A mother gets worried when her children are far away. Take care,

   Mommy

8

"In this passage, Confucius was just allowing his disciple Zigong to find out for himself if the lady in question was indeed pure, by pretending to make advances to her. Contrary to their expectations she resolutely resisted all advances, causing Confucius to express his admiration and respect for the lady. It is my opinion," said our classics professor, "that Confucius treated her unfairly." In our graduation year, his lectures became increasingly unorthodox, so that a lecture on Confucius allowing Zigong to investigate whether "Yon beldam hath the right to speak withal" led to a disquisition on Western sexual liberation. He told us that in the context of the sexual revolution, Zigong should have been making genuine advances to the woman rather than putting her moral integrity to the test. "According to Western views on these matters," the professor asserted, "women who are unmoved by sexual advances are probably frigid."

Nobody was quite sure where he had come by his insights into "Western views on these matters." Students of Western philosophy said he was off-the-wall, and those studying Chinese philosophy said his ideas were a mishmash. Be that as it may, his lectures increasingly became a blend of "discourse on everything but analysis of nothing" and "interpretations of the sexual relations of yin and yang." At times he would even mention himself in the same breath as foreign movie stars.

The classics professor also conducted individual tutorial sessions, an hour a week with each of us. In addition to going through our class work, he would cover ground that was well outside the syllabus. These sessions were pretty easygoing to begin with, but the relaxed atmosphere grew strained later on. On his wall was pasted a scroll bearing the inscription, *A serene heart need not bestir itself.* When he felt serene, he would nod his head beatifically at it, but when he did not feel serene, or did not want to, his spirit would take exception to the inscription. Being as widely read as he was, it was pretty easy for him to refute his inscription when he was in a combative mood. It was only a piece of paper with a few characters written on it, after all, so he could rip it down and tear it to shreds any time he wanted to. But if he did that, what would he do if he ever needed them again to settle his spirit? That scroll was a free tranquilizer, the cheapest psychologist you could hope to find – just one look and you could cool right off.

When I went for tutorials, I would sit facing his scroll, absorbing its wisdom as I listened to the professor talking. But because he was sitting facing me, his mind would be in turmoil.

"We Chinese have always taken the Confucian maxim 'Twixt man and woman, hand should ne'er touch hand' as embodying our traditional view of sexual morality. In fact, the novels *The Golden Lotus* and *The Carnal Prayer Mat* are also a seminal part of the national heritage. Ours is a long and noble history of erotic literature. Indeed, our erotic literature is the precursor of erotic literature worldwide. So why is it that we are today so repressed, so craven, so bigoted?" By this point his mouth was twitching. He pulled an early edition of *The Golden Lotus* from his desk drawer and showed it to me. "Have you read this? It's a classic of erotic fiction, and erotica is central to the Chinese literary tradition."

Of course I didn't dare confess to having read the book ten years before, in case he told the university authorities and got me sent down.

"Umm, I've heard of it, Professor," I admitted. "It's supposed to be very good."

He opened the book and held it out for me to read. It was a section detailing the erotic skills and mutual delight of the nobleman Ximen Qing and the Golden Lotus Pan Jinlian.

"Exquisite style! Brilliant!" The professor's hands were shaking uncontrollably. Maybe it was premature senility.

"Yes, Professor." In point of fact I found it rather hard to follow. My purpose in reading it ten years before was to find out how we got made. I hadn't been in it for the culture. Now, confronted by this man holding the book out to me with shaking hands, I couldn't bring myself to sober perusal of the words on the page before me.

I guessed that the professor was somewhere in his forties – fifty at most. He was studious looking, the image of the bookish scholar depicted in classical paintings. His face never betrayed any emotion; even though he could say and do some pretty shocking things, his face was the mask of calm. It was just his hands that kept shaking. He was regarded as a brilliant scholar and generously treated by the university authorities. Everyone said he was an up-and-comer.

"Chinese erotic paintings are likewise among the earliest of their kind in the world." He straightened up again, this time holding a reproduction of an erotic painting. I sat facing the words *A serene heart need not bestir itself,* too scared to move a muscle.

"Ah, the nobility of Chinese civilization," he murmured. I glanced at the picture and did my best to look erudite.

"Recently I've been studying works of Western philosophy and literature. In their discussions of human nature, they respect human needs, and they analyze sex in a scientific way."

It struck me all of a sudden that he was extremely repressed himself, but then I thought maybe I was being unfair to him.

"Of course, your dissertation, 'Substantiality and Insubstantiality in the Midst of Chaos,' is very fine, lending credence to a view of our entire civilization as apparently substantial but actually insubstantial, or else apparently insubstantial but actually substantial, so that with regard to the sexual aspects . . ." He couldn't keep off sex for long.

I stood up to leave. "Thank you for your instruction, Professor. I'll be back next week."

"Of course, of course."

I took up my books and headed for the door.

"Er – do you have a boyfriend?" he asked suddenly.

"Yes."

"Get on well with him?"

"Yes."

"Planning to get married?"

"No."

"Are you lovers?"

"No!" I wasn't telling him the truth; he was too weird.

"Too bad, really too bad."

"Why?"

"The relationship between the members of a couple is a great blessing, and sexual intercourse is one of the greatest of life's pleasures, a foretaste of heaven. Many of the great philosophies and religions view sex as a vehicle for the attainment of the higher realms of spirituality. It's also a known fact that sexual intercourse cures various illnesses."

I kept edging toward the door.

"Don't go just for a minute. There's something else I have to ask you," he pleaded earnestly. "Young people like you are more enlightened in their thinking, and I'd appreciate some instruction from you."

I was listening.

"I have a girlfriend about your age, or maybe a little younger. Come to think of it, she looks quite like you."

This was too fucking much. He couldn't talk about culture without getting on to sex, and now it's his girlfriend, and he has to drag me in!

"Don't tell my wife, please. My girlfriend is stunning, with beautiful long legs like an American movie star. She's great looking when she's wearing clothes and when she isn't."

So much for his contemporary aesthetics!

"Westerners call girls like her sexy. Asians would say she was – well, Asians don't have any polite names for it." His face was bland and scholarly as ever. "I go and see her every week, and she's just aching for it. With her I finally found out how beautiful sex can be. I keep my wife satisfied – she's crazy for it too, you know – and I have these dates with my girlfriend as well. Women can't take everything I've got for them. I'm tougher than the cowboys in the movie Westerns."

Now he's got Hollywood movies on the brain!

"Don't get me wrong. I hope you'll understand why I'm telling you this. It's because it's so hard to find someone who will understand. I feel you're a broad-minded sort of person, and you're not going to get in a flap about this kind of thing. I can't talk to anyone of my generation this way; they wouldn't appreciate it. Not that they're so pure themselves, the hypocrites! Our generation is pitiful, honestly. When we were young, it was almost a crime for a couple to walk down the street hand in hand. Even after marriage, our sex life was supposed to be as regular and uneventful as the monthly issue of ration coupons. It's only since I started reading Western philosophy these last few years that I realized that we've been living like automatons, wasting our lives. When I took another look back over the history of Chinese civilization, I realized that our ancestors knew how to enjoy life to the full, but the tradition died out somewhere along the way. Now, when you get to our generation, everything we do is regulated for us by the state!

"I'd never given these matters too much thought. The

country was liberated soon after I was born. I didn't do much beside studying when I was young, and I'd hardly spoken to a woman before I started at the university. One of my fellow students was savagely criticized by the Youth League for showing a girl a copy of *The Story of the Stone* and writing her a love letter. My marriage was arranged by the authorities. My wife was a model youth leaguer, and everyone said we were 'perfect help-mates, a revolutionary red couple.' I only kissed her once before the wedding, and that was on the cheek, but it still scared the hell out of her. That's my life for you – I was over forty before I found out what love and romance could be.

"Of course my girlfriend's much more liberated than that. She does things in modern ways. I kiss her whole body, every part of it, including her ———— when she's turned on. . . ." His face was ever so slightly red.

I pulled on my gloves.

"Sometimes I stand. . . ." He had forgotten I was there.

I opened the door.

A couple of days later, someone came from the university authorities to ask me some questions about the classics professor.

"You were his student. Tell us what he talked to you about in tutorials."

"Well there was Master Confucius, Master Mencius, Master Mozi and Master Laozi, Master Confuse-us, Master Monstrous, Master Mousy, and Master Lousy. . . ." I said whatever stupid thing occurred to me.

"What else?"

"Then there were all Confucius' disciples, Little Zigong, Little Zilu, Little Zixi, Little Sir Tom, Little Sir Dick. . . ." I continued in the same vein.

"He must have said something extracurricular, though."

"What do you mean, something? It was *all* extracurricular."

"Things you're not supposed to talk about."

"What aren't we supposed to talk about?"

"Well, Western sexual liberation, sexual freedoms, Freud, *The Golden Lotus*, that kind of thing."

It looked as if he'd been telling everyone about his sex life.

"He only talked about Western philosophy to compare it with Chinese philosophy," I offered.

"What did he say about it?"

"Whatever it was, China always came out on top."

"How about sexual liberation?"

"I forget."

"Okay, but let me just warn you about him. We found pornographic pictures in his briefcase!"

"Really?" The classics professor must have been out of his mind.

"Foreign ones!"

"I wouldn't know. I never saw them." That was a new one on me.

"You really don't know?"

"I really don't know."

"All right. You just think it over for a while, and, if anything occurs to you, you can report it to the organization at any time. We are confident in the ability of the younger generation to tell right from wrong." And my interrogation was over.

The classics professor's love life was the hottest news around. I heard that they were going to throw him out of the Party because of it, and they canceled all his classics courses.

I said, "We get up to all sorts of stuff and nobody investigates us. How come they make such a fuss over the classics professor and his little bit of romance?"

"It's because he wanted too much," said Xiaobo. "He wanted to be a big shot, and he wanted to get away with the other as well. Serves him right."

After I graduated, I used to think about the classics professor every time I saw the book vendors on the streets with all those books about sex. Everyone was desperate to buy *The Golden Lotus,* so much so that even in a bowdlerized edition it fetched the price of a bicycle on the black market. The vendor's shelves were full of books with titles like *Sex and Health, History of Human Sexuality, Female Sexuality and the Orgasm, Sex and the Young* and *Stop Masturbation Now.* I was flipping through a stack of new magazines one day when I came across one with a scholarly article on Taoism by the classics teacher. On the cover was a folksinger in a bikini, and on page 19 there was a photograph of the classics professor and his wife. The caption introduced him as a modest and diligent scholar, spartan and sensitive, of encompassing research and liberated thinking, an upstanding husband and a fine Party member.

On the mild and scholarly face in the picture was the slightest of smiles.

9

So why wasn't I born an ant?

"I think you'd better find someone else to be your husband. I don't see what the big deal is about husbands anyway, but if that's what you want, you'll have to find one somewhere else. That's just not my scene." Yang Fei never looked up from his painting. We'd been living together for ten years. We shared a two-room apartment with his mother, and everyone thought I was sleeping in her room.

As far as my mother and Auntie were concerned, I was a member of his family already, and they were prepared to turn a blind eye to our arrangement on the assumption that we would eventually marry and have a child. None of us had any idea he would come up with this artistic temperament business.

"Painting is my wife; you're my lover," was his last profound word on the subject.

Oh yeah? I moved back in with Mommy and Auntie and told them to find me a man to marry. I was engaged within the week.

"Yang Fei, I'm getting married." I hoped that would shock him.

He laughed. "Go ahead, and good luck to you."

I tried again. "Yang Fei, aren't you afraid I might kill myself?"

He laughed again. "People who talk suicide never do it. Really, I mean it; I wish you well."

Furiously I thought of all the possible ways I might kill

myself, but by the time I'd hit on the best way I'd also decided that it wasn't worth the effort, so I went along to the registry office for the marriage license.

And got married.

The groom's mother was an old friend of my mother's, and they had a lot more in common with each other than I did with my husband.

"Such a fine figure of a man!" said Auntie. "You're a perfect couple!"

I wore a red satin jacket to the wedding. Mommy and the groom's parents started to sing the songs of their heyday in the civil war:

> Chiang Kai-shek, Chiang Kai-shek,
> If we catch him, give him heck.
> He's so funny; let him run; he
> Leaves us all in milk and honey.

They were all giggling away as they sang, as if they were at a party to commemorate their victory over the Nationalists.

> We're two lovers hand in hand
> Off to battle goes my man,

sang the groom's mother, well off-key. Her husband, a former comrade of my father's, offered one of his own:

> Hear the dog go woof! woof! woof!
> Hear the ducks go quack! quack! quack!
> Marching footsteps sound outside
> My Red Army man is back!

Then it was Mommy's turn:

> Across the fields behold fresh blooms of May
> O'er blood-stained earth where gallant
>   soldiers lay.

I wasn't sure whether she was thinking of Daddy or her other darling, but it almost had us all in tears.

In this celebration of revolutionary history, it seemed more like they were the ones getting married.

When my brother had a few drinks, he could get hysterical or depressed, murderous or suicidal. When he was sixteen he had joined the United Action Red Guard battalion for a couple of days, and when they fell out of favor he had spent a month behind bars and emerged with the beginnings of a hunched back. Down in the countryside, his teeth had gone black from the village tobacco, and he had been drunk so often his body reeked. After he came back to a factory job, he lost an eye in a foundry accident when molten metal spat into it. Now he intoned unsteadily,

"Bright moon – hic – when – hic – will there – hic – be wine."

"Auntie, you sing for us," I proposed.

"Oh, no, gracious me, all the songs I know are way out-of-date," Auntie protested.

"Come now, Elder Sister," boomed the groom's father. "The leadership has urged us to let a hundred flowers bloom, let a hundred schools contend. New and old are equally fine, as long as they benefit the Four Modernizations."

"Dad's a pompous asshole," murmured the groom.

Auntie made her contribution: "When I was a girl there was a song the young wives would sing if their husbands weren't playing fair:

If you're not home tonight, my dear
Then get the hell right out of here.

"Dear, dear me, that was a bit on the rude side,"
the groom's mother gasped.

"Great singing," cheered the newlyweds and my brother. My mother-in-law glowered at me.

Old man Song's in the opium trade
Man and wife on the fiddle diddle diddle –

sang my brother provocatively.

I finished his song for him:

– If you want to make the grade
Part *your* hair in the middle diddle diddle.

Mommy shooed us away: "Why don't you go and help in the kitchen?"

That evening, I lay in bed with my new husband, breathing in the heavy varnish of our new furniture and raised the subject of divorce.

"What?" yelled my mother the next day. "Divorce? What's gone wrong?"

"Nothing's gone wrong. We just don't think there's any point going on with it."

"You're going too fast," Mommy complained. "It's not normal."

"Mommy, I promise – "

"What?"

"I promise I'll – " As a child, I had always been able to get out of a spanking by saying "I promise I'll never do it again." On this occasion, it didn't seem the right thing to say somehow. Promise I'll never do what again?

Yang Fei was right about marriage: it does make you hypersensitive.

The best thing I can say for my husband was that he neither loved nor hurt me. He married me to be a good son to his parents – it was all his mother's idea in the first place – and he agreed to a divorce to do the decent thing by me. He had a life of his own to live as well. He venerated women, and they adored him in return.

After we divorced, I started living on my own. Mommy and Auntie would eye me suspiciously up and down every time they saw me. They were of the opinion that I lacked the purity that a single woman ought to have, because I was neither a virgin nor a widow faithful to the memory, nor even a wife waiting loyally like Wang Baochuan. To them I was a hussy divorced from her husband and looking out for a lover. "How could you be a daughter of mine?" ranted Mommy, back in her Anna mode.

The composition teacher in primary school criticized my bluebottle essay and made me change the ending to read, ". . . That fires would consume me! That the sewer would bear me away! That a flyswatter would slap me! . . ." So it goes.

After my dog Dopey drove him away, Yang Fei went off and got married too, but when he was finished with that, he was back to singing me love songs over the phone.

Just before I left the country, Mommy took my hand and told me yet again, "After you were born, the doctors ran all sorts of tests on you, and they said that you were superior to the other babies in all respects."

I knew that she no longer had any hopes for me. She was just saying it to comfort me, and to comfort herself that her giving birth to me had done me no harm.

She stamped her foot feebly. "You're a daughter of the Huang clan, no matter what, and you should always keep your Daddy and me in mind and not let us down."

What was so special about the Huang clan anyway? I did some research into the family tree and discovered that several generations back, one of our ancestors had deserted the army and eloped with a famous beauty. From their union had sprung countless scions of outstanding, if eccentric, talent, but it was not until Daddy that the clan finally produced the man of stature who would truly establish the fortunes of the family, and then *he* had to go and commit suicide. The men of the Huang family all had scholarly faces, and they could sing, dance, ride, and hunt, but because of their unconventional nature, none of them ever amounted to much. A fortune-teller once told one of them that he had a moribund physiognomy. The only real hero was Daddy – until he killed himself, that is. Mommy had hoped that her children would be the ones to restore the family fortunes, but my brother was drunken, abusive, and morose, and I was "wooly headed and spineless." That left Mommy with nothing to do but sit around the house smoking, getting fat and chatting. She and Auntie developed an infinite capacity for talk – Mommy taught Auntie revolutionary dialectics, and Auntie taught Mommy folk religion.

When we were condemned in the Cultural Revolution, the other members of the Huang clan all made a point of drawing a clear dividing line between themselves and us, and making public declarations that they had severed all relations with Daddy. After the Cultural Revolution was over, however, they came to seek us out again. We were deluged by cousins, second cousins and other assorted relations, paying respects, offering to help us out or asking for favors. The year after a flood back home, some distant relative entrusted a young girl to us. The word was that she had been orphaned, and now there was nothing for her to eat because of the flooding, so would Mommy find something for her in the city? The girl was seventeen but looked younger, and Mommy decided to keep her around the house.

They were talking family one day, and the girl said, "Granny, d'you know there was murderers in our family?"

"What!" Mommy practically jumped out of her skin.

"You didn't even know *that?* It was the son of someone or other in the clan – anyways I called him Uncle." Nobody quite knew what blood ties, if any, the girl had with the Huangs, although she was always so full of Granny this and our family that. Certainly none of us had a clue where this uncle of hers fitted in.

"Ooh, it was real gory. He kills this woman. They were at school together. It was all 'cause of the borrowed money, see – never paid it back, so he kills her, and then he chops her up."

"He killed her because she wouldn't pay him back?"

"No, not *his* money; it was *he* got it from *her.*"

"Who borrowed whose money?"

"The man borrows from the girl, see, and he doesn't pay her back."

"How much was it?"

"Oh, I dunno – less than a hundred anyways. She's pushing him to get it back, pushes too hard, and he kills."

"Kills who?" Mommy was a bit confused.

"Kills *her*, right? Kills the *girl*."

"How terrible!"

"And he didn't just chop her up either, he – no, I shouldn't tell you."

"What *did* he do?"

"Well, then he takes the body and – no, I better not."

"Go *on.*"

" – nobbles it."

"What do you mean, *nobble?*" I asked.

"Goodness, child, don't you know anything?" Mommy scolded me. "When folk back home say *nobble* they mean *rape*."

"Yeah, that's it," said the girl. "He rapes her. He wanted to do it before, but she's not having it."

"Who's not having it?"

"The girl. She wouldn't let him, see?"

"Then what?"

"Well he kills her, didn't he, and when she's dead he – " The girl was quite prepared to go through the whole thing again.

"How did he get caught?"

"He nobbles her, right; then he chops bits off her with a meat ax and tosses them into the river. But someone spots her, and they fish her out – ugh, it was really gory."

"Wicked!" Mommy exclaimed.

"Yeah. I saw the bits when they pulled 'em out. Really gross, they was. She was an ugly cow to start with, that one, but hacked about and puffed up she looked worse than ever," the girl concluded.

"Girl, how can you talk like that and not feel morally outraged?"

"What's a moral outrage? I told you she was ugly, didn't I? We all called her Toadface. I dunno why Uncle wanted to borrow her money or screw her."

"Are you sure he was your uncle?" Mommy didn't like admitting to that kind of relative.

"Who knows? He says call me Uncle; I call him Uncle – and he's Uncle if he kills someone or not, and we didn't see nothing so bad about it anyways."

"Why not?" Mommy was totally absorbed.

"'Cause Uncle was so cute. When they took him off to be shot he looked the real hero, like in the movies, you know."

"What did he look like?"

"Like – like Uncle here." The girl indicated my brother.

Mommy nearly passed out.

"Yeah, life's a pain." The girl plowed on, oblivious to her granny's reaction.

"Oh God, the family's ruined," Mommy wailed.

"What d'you mean?" the girl asked.

"Just listen to yourself, how stupid you sound. You don't seem to have had any education at all, and you're supposed to have finished primary." Mommy was looking to vent her anger on the girl.

"Okay, okay," I butted in. "It's all the same however much schooling she's had. What I want to know is, were you scared when your house was flooded?"

"Oh, that was real fun. Everything goes under, just a sheet of water, all white, real neat." The girl got excited at the thought.

So much for my family.

Eggs and rice, eggs and rice,
Eat them once and eat them twice;
Open wide, here they come,

Right into your tum-tum-tum.
Poo your pants, poo your pants;
Wash 'em in the river if you get the chance.
Up your pants froggies come,
Bite you on your bum-bum-bum.

10

Dearest Haha,

I came back to China thinking I was going to make a new start, but I don't know how to begin. . . .

People leave, come back, leave again. Xiaobo has given up his inheritance, closed his psychological counseling service and gone to Australia to undergo what he calls reform through labor. He says he and his girlfriend are going to prove themselves by making it from scratch.

The peasants are all building themselves big houses, but they won't install toilets or bathrooms. They still hold to the custom of digging a pit away from the house even if they have to freeze their butts off to use it. Yang Fei says that ours is a culture that is obsessed with eating but refuses to think about shitting. . . .

I sometimes think I want to have a baby, but I've heard that childbirth is hell. I have a friend who just had a baby girl, and when she was giving birth, the doctor hauled the baby out with forceps so that her head looked like an eggplant. . . .

You want to know what it's like here? I'll give you a list, and you'll know: skyscrapers, fancy hotels, supermarkets, fast-food joints, joint ventures, new policies, epidemics, nepotism, nude art shows, superstars, door-to-door salesmen, export permits, arranged marriages, perfect couples, rock 'n' roll, elopement, prostitution, black-market fiction, modernism, human-meat dumplings, private cars, female infanticide, prophylactic dentistry, tourists, money changers, black-market U.S. dollars, TV ads, firearms, factories, wars, henpecked husbands, abduction and sale of women, female professors, female authors, single-parent families, Kentucky Fried Chicken, Coca-cola, fashion, consumer durables, prizewinning movies, getting rich quick, tours, holidays . . .

How do you make a new start anyway?

Little Jiang

Dear Haha,

You can't be serious about agreeing to Mommy and Auntie marrying themselves off to two old farts they've never even met? What are the Huangs coming to? Even my own son isn't called Huang but has his mother's surname. This is because my mother-in-law insisted on our being "democratic" and "respecting the wishes of the mother." Where's the bloody democracy in that? They tricked me by saying that when we were allowed to have another son we could call that one Huang, but it looks like the one-child policy is here to stay. Seems the Huangs are all washed up.

You remember that girl who showed up saying she was from the ancestral home? She just ran off with a bunch of kids who came back from the countryside. Nobody knows where she is, and we think she's taken our copy of *The Red and the Black*.

How's the weather in London?

Your brother

Dear Haha,

Women are weird. Wedding invitation enclosed.

Old Gu

Antonia?

Haha finally woke up.

The phone was ringing. She picked up the receiver.

"Hey, Haha." It was Liu Ding.

"How're you doing?"

"Did you get the invite?"

"Amazing, eh?"

"Fantastic!"

"Fantastic here too!"

"How so?"

"I'm pregnant!"

"Who's the father?"

"He's married."

"What?"

"I'm going to have the baby."

"What?"

"Going to have the baby, bastard or not!"

"You sure you know what you're doing?"

"It'll be chaos and all that, no point thinking about it."

"What'll you do after?"

"After? To be a woman is to be a mother; to love is to sacrifice; copulation is procreation; self-denial is – "

"Okay, okay. Spare me the bullshit. Just go ahead and have the kid!"

"So what are you doing?"

"Me?" Haha started tearing up the manuscript of her novel. "An old monk telling a story – "

"More bullshit."

Haha ripped the sheets to shreds one by one.

* * *

Meanwhile, at the other end of the world, Auntie was watching storytelling:

"Our story tells us more of that angelic countenance: that such a handsome youth should grace the world! But hidden behind that hypocritical smile was a treacherous seducer. 'I sense your spirit is in some other realm, Master Fang. If you truly love, then I could arrange your union as man and wife.' As soon as Li Huiniang heard these words, she looked back and saw the old villain in a fury. The beautiful maiden was so alarmed that her heart beat fast, her flesh went cold, her face went sallow, and her soul fled her body . . . ," recited the drum singer. Auntie sat glued to the TV, bobbing her head to the beat.

"Let's watch this week's episode of *Anna Karenina.*" Mommy switched channels and broke in on Auntie's reverie.

"Nasty foreign stuff, all mush and romance," Auntie complained.

"Same with all your old operas, isn't it? Just different language."

"Foreigners are ugly."

"They don't look so bad if you see them more often." Haha's mother got in close to the television to watch *Anna.*

"Ugly things. Bushy eyebrows and big eyes, ugh!" Auntie turned away and headed for the kitchen.

Forget about the distance between China and the rest of the world. Please don't get upset with the book and ask me if it's true that the Chinese kill cats and insult each other. And don't ask me if this is the story of my life.

I can tell you this: the Chinese kill everything, just the same as you do. Cursing and insulting each other in all sorts of different ways is part of the Chinese civilization.

And this is certainly not an autobiography, or some historical epic. It's just a collection of scenes and verses, dancing hand in hand in circles large and small. When the circle is complete, the dancers laugh and call it a day.

Liu Sola
New York, November 1993

Chaos and All That is the first fiction written in self-imposed exile by the Chinese composer, rock-singer, playwright, actress, and author Liu Sola. It was written in London and completed in the spring of 1989. After several revisions, the novel was published in Hong Kong in 1991, but it has yet to appear in China, where Liu Sola is known for popular and controversial stories written between 1985 and 1988.

Born in 1955 to an official family in decline, Liu Sola is the niece of Liu Zhidan, a general in the communist Red Army before his death in 1936. Sola's father, Liu Jingfan, had fought alongside his brother and reaped the reward of high office in the newly established Communist regime after 1949. When Liu Zhidan's former comrade Gao Gang was purged in 1955, the Liu family suffered by association, with Liu Jingfan suffering demotion to an insignificant but nonetheless comfortable sinecure. The family's fortunes declined further after the Cultural Revolution erupted in 1966; a fictionalized biography of Liu Zhidan by Sola's mother, Li Jiantong, was denounced by Communist Party chairman Mao Zedong. Li Jiantong was sent to work in a piggery, Liu Jingfan was jailed, and Sola, her brother, and her sister were left in the care of a loyal family retainer. Sola briefly joined the Red Guards but was thrown out because of her family's humiliation.

After the Cultural Revolution ended, Sola passed the 1977 entrance examination for the Central Conservatory of Music, where she studied composition, producing a piano suite inspired by China's earliest poetry collection, *The Book of Songs,* and a symphony dedicated to her famous uncle. After graduation, she turned her attention to pop and rock music, recording three albums of her own songs as well as writing music for film, theater, and television. In 1988, the year she left China, she completed a rock opera version of her novella *Blue Sky Green Sea*.

Liu Sola is one of the most productive of the group of young Chinese writers and artists active in China in the 1980s who found themselves separated, some remaining in China and others scattered outside their homeland, after the brutal suppression of the democracy movement in the summer of 1989. While in England, Sola worked as a writer, singer, composer, and dramatist. In addition to writing *Chaos* and other short fiction, she also created and performed the 1990 theater piece *Memories of the Middle Kingdom*, in which a pair of unsuspecting Englishmen are dragged through an absurdist version of the Cultural Revolution. In 1992, she was a visiting writer at the International Writing Program at the University of Iowa; she also composed a modern dance score based on the classic Chinese opera *Snow in Midsummer* for the choreographer Chiang Ching. Since moving to New York in 1992, she has finished work on a CD recorded with American musicians called *China Blues*.

The tumultuous events of Sola's early years form the backdrop to *Chaos and All That*. Numerous biographical clues link the author to her protagonist Huang Haha: their ages are the same (eleven years old in 1966); both are the daughters of high-ranking officials attacked early in the Cultural Revolution; and both are expelled from the Red Guards because of their families. Even their names are similarly eccentric: Liu is Sola, as in *do-re-mi-fa,* while Huang is named Haha, for the sound of laughter.

We learn little of London in *Chaos*; certainly nothing to compare with, say, Buchi Emechita's depiction of the immigrant experience in *Second Class Citizen,* or Lao She's 1930s comedy of English and Chinese manners, *The Two Mas.* What is important for Sola and Haha alike is where they are not. The Peking of memory overwhelms the London of the moment, making it seem like a lesser reality. Recollections of childhood, youth, pet-ownership, love, and the briefest of marriages are juxtaposed in an absurdist tapestry with discussions of art, sex, and murder. To these are added snippets of poetry ranging from classical forms through revolutionary anthems to doggerel and pop lyrics; there is even a literati-style poetry competition, albeit with a feminist twist, at which the participants adapt an operatic aria to reflect upon their lives.

Liu Sola draws liberally from the literary and documentary sources that influenced her as she grew up in an elite family in the early years of the People's Republic of China. Naturally we see the revolutionary rhetoric of the Communist Party, and the heroes provided for the young to emulate: Chairman Mao's good soldier Lei Feng, endlessly performing good deeds and recording them in his diary, or Liu Wenxue, martyred as he protected a collective vegetable plot from the wicked landlord. Then there is Mao's poetry and the works of Lu Xun, the short-story writer and essayist active in the twenties and thirties who was lionized by Mao. In addition, we can find older cultural traditions: there are references to the great novels of the Ming dynasty (1368–1644) – the Peach Garden Oath sworn by the heroes of *Three Kingdoms,* the prodigious Wu Song of *The Water Margin,* the salacious novel of manners *The Golden Lotus* (still unavailable in China in its unexpurgated form), and the more openly pornographic novel, *The Carnal Prayer Mat.* The young Haha is at least slightly familiar with the greatest of Chinese novels, *The Story of the Stone* (also known as *The Dream of the Red Chamber*), written in the eighteenth century and best known for the troubled romance between its hero Baoyu and his delicate cousin Daiyu. Daiyu's lament for falling blossoms is inadequately remembered by Haha as she dances in her new dress for Auntie (the poem in the novel is twice the length). Finally, there are the heroines served up as models from myth and the operatic tradition: wronged wives like Meng Jiangnü, whose tears for a dead husband threatened to wash away the Great Wall, Li Huiniang, who returned as a ghost to revenge herself on her brutal lord, or Qin Xianglian, who protested her husband Chen Shimei's unfaithfulness to the upright Judge Bao; the celebrated woman general of the Yang family who took on military leadership after her husband's death; and Wang Baochuan, waiting loyally for a husband unjustly banished to serve in military campaigns.

With all these disparate models presented to the young, especially young women, of Liu Sola's generation, is it any wonder that one of the participants in the Committee to Write New Works about Wang Baochuan asks, "How can we live right?" The women of Liu Sola's generation were raised by their families to be studious and infinitely loyal to their parents and future husbands; then, just as they were coming to physical maturity and searching for their own identitiy, they were commanded by their political leaders to overthrow China's traditional culture and spearhead the world revolution. Liu Sola offers no answer to the question of how to live right, but she demonstrates the confusion well enough.

The novel's language, like the narrative, involves the juxtaposition of disparate elements. There is Peking slang, amply laced with profanity and scatology (a searching test for the translator), polemic and bureaucratese, the classical and the operatic, rock lyrics from China and the United States. An illustration of the variations in stylistic level is provided by the Chinese title *Hundun jia li-ger-leng. Hundun* is an ancient term for that primordial chaos that preceded all things. The word is found in the Taoist philosopher Zhuangzi's parable of innocence destroyed, in which the mythological emperor Hundun dies after being given the bodily apertures that make him human. *Hundun* is linked (*jia* meaning simply "plus" or "and") to the Peking slang term *li-ger-leng*. As the author explains it, *li-ger-leng* has three levels of meaning: (1) these are the syllables customarily used to vocalize instrumental accompaniment for operatic singing; thus, by extension, (2) the term is used by the young to describe the speech of those so old and unhip as to like opera; leading to the definition uppermost in Sola's mind, (3) bullshit.

What holds these disparate narrative and linguistic elements together is a comical sense of the absurd. Received truths are lampooned, values are scorned, dignity is deflated, myths are subverted, and momentous events are trivialized. It was precisely this irreverent nihilism that gained for Liu Sola a following among an alienated youth in mid-eighties China and the disapproval of authorities still hoping for a return to the optimistic and loyalist writing of the Maoist era. Addressing Sola's pre-*Chaos* stories and the writing of some of her modernist contemporaries, one Chinese critic condemned them as "irrationalist." The qualities the critic singles out as particularly objectionable in Sola's case are ones of which the author herself would probably be proud: the futility of Albert Camus (in *The Myth of Sisyphus*), the frustration of Joseph Heller's *Catch-22,* the plotlessness of Samuel Beckett's *Waiting for Godot,* and the narrative voice of Liu Sola's favorite character in American fiction, Holden Caulfield in J. D. Salinger's *The Catcher in the Rye.* Sola believes that with *Chaos* she has developed a voice that is more distinctively her own and owes less to other writers she admires; still, we can expect that orthodox critics may be further outraged, and lovers of the absurd further delighted, when *Chaos* is finally unleashed on a Chinese audience.

My initial translation of *Chaos* was made from the author's first manuscript draft; it was subsequently revised as the author rewrote parts of the novel. I would like to thank Liu Sola for her full and delightful answers to questions put to her about her life and work, Antony Harwood for suggesting the English title, and Tu Wei, Daniel Bryant, Steve Jones, and two anonymous readers engaged by the University of Hawaii Press for their comments on the translation.

Beijing, December 1993

Production Notes

Composition and paging were done in
Framemaker software on an AGFA
Accuset Postscript Imagesetter by
the design and production staff of
University of Hawaii Press.

The text and display typeface is Garamond.

Offset presswork and binding were done by
The Maple-Vail Book Manufacturing Group.
Text paper is Glatfelter Offset Vellum,
basis 50.